AFTER IT H

BOOK 2: HUMANITY

DEVON C FORD

Originally self-published by Devon C Ford in 2016

Published by Vulpine Press in the United Kingdom in 2017

ISBN: 978-1-910780-22-0

www.vulpine-press.com

Dedicated to the real Leah, who kicks ass in her own way.

PROLOGUE

Dan woke and opened his eye to an ornate but unfamiliar high ceiling.

He could only see from his right side, however. He raised a tentative hand to feel his face, discovering heavy bandaging to the forehead and left side. The events flooded back to him, and the tears of grief and fear started to fall weakly for the loss of his friends.

"He's awake!" shrieked a voice which could only belong to Leah. The noise lanced through him like a bullet, tearing him from his self-pity.

Too many people to count rushed in, staring at him. He turned his painfully stiff neck to his right to see only one other bed occupied. Everyone tried to speak to him at once until Kate's commanding voice cut through the cacophony to berate them all and banish them from the medical wing.

She came to him, shining a light in his eye and asking him questions to assess his level of concussion.

He answered them all groggily, then started with his own. "What happened?" was the best he could do. His throat was sore and his mouth dry.

"You caused merry bloody hell, that's what happened," she said, reading his mind and bringing a bottle of water with a straw in. "Running off like you did to play cowboy."

Her words were softened by her genuine smile at seeing him conscious and mostly whole.

"They argued all night about going after you. In the end, Jack said he heard something on the radio, so we just went," she said plainly.

"We?" he croaked.

"Joe, Jack, Neil and me," she replied. "Found you slumped in Lexi's truck and found the others parcelled up inside," she continued, and before he had a chance to ask, "both are fine. Lexi is still out," she gestured to the bed beside him, "but she is responding normally. Serious concussion, and she needed some stitches. Lots of stitches, actually. Steve was let out yesterday. He was the only one of you not to have a glass jaw, by the way, but he got twenty-six stitches in the arm. You got nearly forty on your head because I had to be more delicate to maintain your rugged good looks." She waited for a laugh and realised one wasn't coming.

Dan started to cry silently, remembering the one name that hadn't been mentioned.

Kate went on, "I can't comment on the last patient, as I'm underqualified." She let that sink in.

He turned his good eye to her. "Ash?" he asked, hopeful.

"Leah!" she called towards the closed door. "I know you're out there. Be useful and go and find Sera."

No reply was heard, but the door opened a couple of minutes later.

"Sorry for the delay," Sera announced happily as she entered. "I've been training this little shit to not bite me. Everyone else is fair game as far as I'm concerned, but I had to muzzle him before he gave up and let me stitch him."

Ash limped towards Dan on three legs as fast as he could, his tail wagging ludicrously and threatening to destabilise him. He jumped on the bed and tried to lick Dan through the confines of the muzzle.

"How?" Dan asked, but he could not continue.

"They found you outside," said Sera. "They found the others where you had left them. You were all brought back here."

He looked at her, holding on to his dog tightly and looking at the shaved patch of fur where a series of ragged stitches held together the slashed skin on his left shoulder.

"Joe went inside to see what had happened. I'm told he has stopped being sick now. He brought back all of your stuff and afterwards followed the last trail of blood to where he found this recalcitrant mutt barking at a window out of his reach. He had lost plenty of blood, but let me tell you, he was still damned difficult to catch even on three legs." She rolled up her left sleeve to show a series of bruises and puncture wounds. "Don't worry about me," she said with mock selflessness, "I'm only on a course of antibiotics and had to have a tetanus booster in the arse, much to her delight." She shot a playfully evil look at Kate, who blew her a kiss. "Seriously, though, he was going to have us all until he saw you in here. We had to show you to him every hour or so when he started to play up. You need to sort that out."

Dan was so happy that they had made it out alive that he forgot to ask about the one who had nearly killed all four of them.

"I need to see Joe, now," he said, suddenly serious.

3

Joe bustled in, full of self-importance, only seconds after a shouted summons. He must have been in Ops.

"Welcome back, boss," he said.

Dan owed him a lot, and decided to play it nice. "You did well, Joe. Tell me what you found."

Joe told the story Dan had already heard from Kate and Sera. Joe had gone in and followed the same tracks which were blatantly obvious, as Dan had left a wide smear of blood as he dragged out the other two. It was mostly them who had smeared Dan's blood, but still, it was like following a satnav, Joe said. He found the candlelit room and recovered all the weapons, as well as Lexi's shredded equipment. He heard barking and followed it to where he found Ash on three legs with barely the energy to stand. He refused to leave a window that was covered in bloodstains, and he had to send someone back to fetch Sera and Chris, who eventually managed to get a blanket over Ash and subdue him with minimal injury.

To themselves.

Sera had stitched up the dog while Kate, Alice and Lizzie had stitched up the people, and there they all were. Kate was especially proud that Alice had done her first sutures and supervised her treatment of Steve's wound, as it was the easiest to stitch. Dan's face required more experienced hands, apparently, including their resident veterinarian's.

"Joe," Dan said carefully, "what about *him*?" he asked.

"No trace, boss. Went out the window and vanished. Missing Lexi's knife, but I found everything else," he said.

Joe left, and Dan turned to face the still-sleeping Lexi.

"I'm bloody starving. How long have I been out?" he asked Kate.

"Two days," she said, bringing coffee and food.

THE HEALING PROCESS

Lexi woke that afternoon and immediately began to scream, arching her back like she was having a fit. Kate and Lizzie ran to settle her. Dan felt helpless and responsible for her pain.

"You're officially discharged," Kate told Dan, summarily dismissing him from the makeshift ward as she charged a hypodermic syringe with what he suspected was morphine.

Alice helped him walk from his bed to his own room. Ten metres had not felt so tiring since he had dragged the two unconscious Rangers from the hospital.

He found that his cot was gone and a proper double bed had been put in his room, with a real quilt, and he was propped up on it.

"Courtesy of Jimmy," Alice said.

Sera appeared not long after and delivered Ash, now without the muzzle. The dog climbed onto the bed with difficulty and settled down to sleep after his renewed excitement had tired him.

Leah came in not long after bearing plastic plates of food and sat with him to eat as she shared news from the last two days.

Nobody had been out since they had returned; it seemed like they were locked down until further notice. Joe had stood guard throughout the day, with others taking shifts to remain awake at night.

The world continued to turn, it seemed, without his permanent presence to organise people. Steve joined them, prompting Dan to ask Leah to take some time off. She skipped away, eager to warm up with some TV time and whatever it was she got up to.

He asked Steve to open the window and pass him his cigarettes, which he did. Dan inhaled deeply as he relished the taste and feel of the nicotine in his lungs. Ash grumbled and shifted position, but did not complain any further at his bad habit.

Steve thanked him for what he did, prompting Dan to wave his thanks away as irrelevant. Steve's left arm was bandaged and in a sling, but Dan saw that he wore a sidearm on his right hip and sported three spare magazines on his belt.

Steve had cleaned the ugly shotgun belonging to Dan and put it on a small shelf above Dan's head where the cigarettes and a plastic bowl to use as an ashtray went.

A short time after, Neil brought in a wheeled trolley with a TV and DVD on, plugging it into a long lead connected to his bank of generators.

It seemed that people's comfort and entertainment were more important than conserving petrol right now.

He watched some awful, far-fetched films over the rest of the day. It seemed that people could drive cars between consecutive skyscrapers, without injury, and still be able to deliver sensational one-liners.

He had various visitors, all ignored by Ash, who still slept noisily. He was brought snippets of news until he had built a picture of how the civilian contingent was coping in the absence of their warrior class. Chris still worked the farm with Sera keeping a watchful eye when she wasn't moonlighting as a human doctor, and Cedric and Maggie were busy over on the gardens. Both Chris and Cedric now carried shotguns as provided by Pete from the civilian armoury. This was apparently done on Penny's instruction, and Joe was forbidden to leave the grounds until more Rangers were fit.

He struggled to the toilet that afternoon as his newly employed digestive system kicked in. Ash wanted to stay asleep, and Dan managed a short trip outside to walk – or, more accurately, hobble – his dog before bed.

More food and more news were brought to him throughout the evening, before he was given more tablets and a healthy dose of Scotch before he slept.

The following morning, Sera came to walk Ash before breakfast, and he responded with stiffness and grumbling before he gave up and sat to have her put a lead around his neck.

Breakfast came next, brought by Leah, who had charged an iPad she had borrowed from one of the others and wanted to play a game of air hockey with Dan, which was more like pong. He tried to explain pong to Leah and gave up.

At lunchtime, he was visited by Kate and Sera and examined; they said he would be fine and left more tablets with a bottle of water.

Jay came next and lit a fire in his room, changing the atmosphere considerably. Neil had closed his window mostly, but given him a pipe to blow smoke down for it to escape outside.

That evening, Lexi was helped into his room, where she was propped up alongside Dan and left. They sat in silence and watched another blockbuster, seemingly chosen as a radical form of PTSD cure. Halfway through *I am Legend*, when the dog died, they both cried unashamedly and both received annoyed and confused looks from Ash.

Hours after they were put together, they began to speak about the hospital.

"I'm so sorry–" Dan said.

Lexi cut him off and told him bluntly, "I knew the risks of being a Ranger; it was just unlucky that he got the drop on me."

Dan thought that it was more than luck. He had "got the drop" on two trained men after he took her out, then wounded a vicious animal intent on ripping his throat out before escaping.

"He wasn't lucky; he was possessed. Driven mad by all this shit. He was dangerous and he and others like him may still be out there," said Dan, unintentionally bringing the mood down to minus ten degrees.

Lexi didn't say anything for a while, but he knew she was doing some soul-searching. She lacked the words to express it yet, but she had had a near miss. A very near miss.

"Thank you for coming to save me," she said quietly. "I don't know what he was going to do, but they told me what he had done when I was knocked out. I'd have rather died than go through whatever he planned. I'm glad I didn't." She smiled at him, ever a lamb in his flock, it seemed. He didn't know how to respond.

"There's space; can I just stay where I am tonight instead of going back to medical?" she asked hopefully.

He wanted her to, but didn't want her to misunderstand the reasons. "Yeah, but if your farts are bad and you snore, then you're out. That's the dog's job," he said, receiving a disdainful look from Ash.

They drank and watched another DVD afterwards, but the generator power was cut and they both fell asleep in silence and darkness.

MINORITY OF ONE

He had pulled himself desperately through the window as the hideous animal snapped at him, eager for more of his flesh.

He fell to coldness and safety on the outside, clutching at the ragged mess on his right side. He ran to a place he knew well and slumped into the corner, where he lay shivering throughout the night.

The third great lance of flame and noise from the man's gun had torn a big scrap of flesh away above the patient's right hip. He was pressing his badly mangled left hand into the ragged wound. He could not move those fingers anyway. He looked down and saw that the ligaments and tendons of the back of his hand were all exposed, some severed and bunched tight, never to be of use again.

He hurt everywhere; that evil animal had bitten him many times until he had managed to stick it with the knife.

He lay there, waiting for the demon to tell him what to do, but no instructions came. No commands to follow were given.

What did come was an ever-increasing weakness, and the puddle of congealing blood around him widened.

His breathing became shallow and fast.

He realised that the demon had abandoned him, that he was not strong enough to transcend as promised.

He was not worthy, which was why he was going to die.

He was cold. Tears of sadness and weakness, of impotent rage and loneliness, began to fall from his eyes.

As his breathing became sporadic and his heart finally ran out of blood to pump around his body, he lost consciousness.

The patient died where he sat in the corner of his old room in the secure wing of the psychiatric hospital, surrounded by the rotting bodies of those who gave him the tablets which had kept the demon away for so long.

FREEDOM IS THE RIGHT TO TELL PEOPLE WHAT THEY DO NOT WANT TO HEAR

As decided, nobody went off the reservation save for those who tended to the gardens twice a week. All the preparations for winter had been done with nothing to plant until the new year. The horses and sheep had been moved to the farm, so all the animals were in close proximity for wintering.

A crude system of rainwater collection provided water to the bathrooms via the guttering; this saved having to carry up bottled water to use for washing, thereby extending their water resources further.

Penny came to see him the next day, and he insisted on dressing and meeting her in Ops with a gun at his waist. He had not spoken to her since before the hospital, and he was not happy about the whisperings he had been hearing from his covert sources; he had to appear strong in front of her, despite his injuries.

It had been said that Penny wanted control of the Rangers to come under her department and not be run separately by Dan. The rumours spoke of a political coup, of a subtle but important balance of power.

Still quite shaky on his feet and with half of his head bandaged, he walked tall and asked Leah for a report as he strode into Ops.

"All quiet," she said.

"Penny," Dan said in greeting, turning his head to be able to see her. She was flanked by her new PA, Karen.

"May we talk?" asked Penny quietly.

"Leah? Break time," he said, and the girl walked from the room with as much dignity as she could muster in the circumstances. She knew full well when she was being dismissed for grown-up talk. She clicked her fingers to Ash, who followed without question –following his stomach, Dan thought.

He sat at the main table with the two women, and he turned to look pointedly at Karen.

"Would you give us the room, please?" Penny said politely to the woman after following his deliberate gaze. Karen looked surprised, even a little affronted, but gathered her things and left the room in a mimic of Leah but without the same level of grace and decorum.

This obviously wasn't a meeting that required minutes.

The two looked at each other for a few seconds in silence before Penny broke first.

"How have we come to regard each other like this?" she asked.

He wasn't sure how to explain it without causing offence, so he didn't bother to try. "Our ideal was a cooperative society, which you are trying to turn into a communist state," he said.

Penny bridled instantly, and Dan thought she would rise and leave the room. She kept her temper in check and answered him acidly. "That is ridiculous and slanderous," she bit back. "You would turn us into a *police* state with martial law, I presume?" She emphasised the word police, and left the counter-accusation hanging heavily.

"Without protection, where would we be?" he asked rhetorically. "Rules are protection. Coordination is safety. We all have our jobs here, and mine is to deal with the violence so you and the others don't have to. You think me barbaric, but you misunderstand me intentionally. We are the rough men who stand ready," he said, meaning to get through to her on a deeper level with references to literature. "The violence I use is for the good of all and not myself," he finished, having risen from his seat as he spoke to lean his hands on the table.

His aching head hurt as he spoke, but he could not show weakness now.

"There is, and will be, no police state here. No Big Brother," he said more quietly as he sat back down and seemed to shrink in size, "which means there will be no inequality also. No leadership class of person to rule the others. We work together or we are all slaves."

"What are we, if not the leading class?" asked Penny. "You lead yours for now and I lead mine, so what is the difference?"

This was too much for Dan. "There is a world of difference!" he shot back vehemently, ignoring the "for now" comment. "We lead because we are the best placed in our fields. When someone better comes along, they will lead instead of us. No one person should have the final say. Your model of our cooperative society is a dictatorship and nothing more!"

Penny said nothing, so he carried on. "What if a member of the group wished to take a council seat? Maybe yours? What then? Would you have a Ranger banish them? Punish them? Would you have us performing public executions?"

Penny stuttered for words, unable to admit that she had never given a thought to relinquishing power.

"They must be allowed to present their case to everyone, others would present their own and the people will decide. If another person wanted my job, they could have it, but they would have to prove to everyone that they are better at it than I am. I will not retain power by force, nor will I wield it to keep you on your damned pedestal," he finished angrily.

Penny was fuming, but silent. He knew he had said some things that shocked her, mostly because they were true and she would not admit it to herself. She was also angry that he knew more than she thought he did. Obviously, her quiet plays for power amongst the wider group had reached ears sympathetic to Dan's popularity.

Dan stood, slowly and carefully pushing his chair back under the table, before fixing Penny with his good eye. "Please, Penny," he said softly. "Remember how we all started this journey together. I don't want overall control, but I will challenge you for it if needs be. Please, this is about all of us and not just one person. There's no throne, no crown here. It's survival or death, and if we fight amongst ourselves, then there won't be much in the way of survival."

He walked out, wanting to lie down again for a very long time but feeling too wound up to stay still. He walked slowly outside and sat heavily on a felled tree trunk some distance away, deep in thought.

It was there that Leah found him. He had no idea how long he'd been there until his trance was interrupted by the girl and his dog. She sat next to him in silence.

"What we do now will inevitably change us," he said softly to her. To himself. "What we see and do will take whatever innocence we have left, and our humanity with it. To survive, we have to adapt, to adopt the same behaviour as the people we fight." He hung his head with a sigh and continued the introspection. "We have to become capable of rage and the sickening violence we see them use, but there is a difference."

The last word he said with savage passion. He turned to the silent girl, seeing his own bright eyes mirrored in hers as she let his words soak in.

"The difference is that we keep our evil locked away deep inside us until we need it, and then we let it out of the cage to protect what we have. We let it out to get the job done and then we lock it away again."

He hung his head again and sighed, the sudden fire now extinguished.

"But there is a cost to us. We're not monsters but we have to act like monsters, and that takes a toll on us. We are willing to make that sacrifice to keep people safe. To make life peaceful."

He got up, dizzy for a second with a wave of pain and exhaustion.

"You're right," he said to Leah, who still hadn't spoken a word. "OK. I'll talk to Penny again," he said as he rose with difficulty, leaving her sitting there.

WHYS AND WHEREFORES

Penny returned to her room and paced restlessly. She had been so scared when Dan had gone chasing after Lexi, and felt awful for relishing the thought that he might not come back alive or at all. She imagined herself moulding his replacement into a more malleable version of him: a controllable leader of her personal honour guard.

Dan's words had cut her deeply. Her temper was high, and made worse when she realised that he was right about her behaviour. The truth was, she was enjoying the power.

It started as happiness to have other people, then swelled into pride to have people working for her. The routine of giving orders and thinking of jobs for people to do, then choosing who should do them, had taken over her every waking thought. So much so that without realising it, she had accrued a staff to follow her around and annotate those orders for distribution.

She had grown power-hungry, and she was suddenly ashamed at the realisation.

It wasn't intentional, she convinced herself. It was the situation: it did things to people. From the very beginning she had busied herself every day, and when more people joined them, she had more to organise and so on and so forth. She told herself that they all needed her to plan their every day. They wouldn't be on the firm ground they were had it not been for her leadership.

Sometimes that leadership took away the choices of the people, but it was for their own good. People came to her with ideas, with suggestions, and she politely listened at first. Lately she had been so busy that she started to turn them away.

Since Karen arrived, she had issued a standing order not to be disturbed directly, and for Karen to take the details of those wanting to see her. She had become obsessive, almost fanatical in her thoughts of the future, for reasons she hadn't shared with anyone she now knew.

She stopped pacing and stood still. She started to cry. She was suddenly so very tired, she thought as she lay down on her bed to submit to the sobs coming from deep inside her. She felt sick, and the waves of pain that had affected her recently started again.

A while later, Dan found her still in that position. He sat gently on the edge of her bed and rested his left hand lightly on her shoulder. She woke to see him watching her, and for once did not have the energy to straighten her appearance.

"I am so sorry," she said. "Things just took on a momentum that I couldn't–"

"It's OK," he said. "We need you to be you, nothing more."

She smiled and closed her eyes again.

RUMOUR CONTROL

All of them sat together for dinner at the tables. They ate, and afterward Dan told them the sanitised version of events at the hospital. He thanked the people he wanted to thank, and laid out some ground rules with a heavy olive branch.

"Penny's direction to have those on the farm and gardens carrying shotguns is to remain in place. Anyone wanting training is to make themselves known," he said. "On that note," he continued, "suggestions and questions are more commonplace now that there are lots of us." He paused to scan the room, having to raise his voice for all of them to hear him. "These will be written down – we have plenty of paper – and placed in the box that Karen will organise. We will bring these to the council every week. Concerns about everyday work are to be brought to your head of department, but this provides another route which should be available as we have agreed." He nodded to Penny, who graciously accepted the mention even though nothing of the sort was decided until Dan said it now.

"We are locking down things for the winter, so everyone is going to have more time on their hands. There will be three hours of electricity after dinner from the generators. My advice is not to let Leah choose the film every night." That got the laughs he hoped for.

"Over the next week, everyone is to find a time to report to Kate so that the medical unit have a full history and everyone gets an MOT." Another ripple of low laughter. He had discussed this with

Kate, Lizzie and Alice and they had been preparing a filing system to keep medical notes on them all.

"Nobody will go off site unless with permission, not counting those working on the farms and gardens. Or Pete, obviously," he added.

"There will only be a couple of trips made a month during the worst weather, and until our wounds are healed, there won't be any. So everyone take some time to relax. Those of you organised to help with the farm know who you are; this gives farm workers time off to make it fair."

He asked Leah what the film was tonight, and she said a title he didn't recognise, which prompted a mixture of different noises from the rest of them. The group took that as dismissal, and he nodded to his operations department when he got their eye contact. He had to call Leah over, and she came reluctantly holding a DVD which he could only describe as "pink". He decided to deal with her job first so she could get on with having a life.

"Any applications coming in to Ops go to you, you record them in a ledger and keep them ready to discuss. OK?" he said.

"OK. What's a ledger?" she asked.

"A book used to keep lists," he said, keeping it simple to avoid the trademark "wait, what?" from her again.

She ran off hoping to get to the TV before someone overrode her film choice. He sat down to look around his Rangers, and what he saw was almost pitiful. He still had half of his face bandaged and had not yet seen the damage. He had, however, seen the grimace on Kate's face when she changed the dressings. Steve was still bandaged, but he had lost the sling. Joe was uninjured but was still the weakest link, as bad as Dan felt by thinking it. Lexi was badly bruised over her head and face. Her eyes were ringed with purple and yellow, and she moved stiffly under a loose sweatshirt. He knew the cuts on her chest were worse than she made out. It would probably be weeks before they were all fully fit, and he had to look at a rehabilitation programme for them. They needed to stay fit and lean. There was no off-season training or warm-up games – when they went out, they had to be at one hundred per cent or people would die.

"Sidearms at all times, we'll take a day at a time each in Ops. Joe, me, Steve, Lex, in that order. When we are physically capable, we are making a trip that will require some heavy machinery." Eyebrows were raised. "Police armoury – hopefully more Glocks, MP5s, G36s. If we're really lucky, they've upgraded to the HK416s. Either way, we need more guns that aren't for pheasant shooting."

Agreement all round, although there were some questioning looks about his knowledge.

Dan stayed to help clear the plates as he realised that Cara was waiting behind in the kitchen, heating the water to wash up and not wanting to interrupt. He apologised and helped her. They talked as they worked; Dan washed and Cara dried up, and she promised to make a lemon drizzle cake for him – one of the small echoes of sentimentality which he felt mattered.

He walked outside the front door and lit a cigarette as Ash limped around in circles looking for the best place to empty his bladder. Lexi joined him, as he suspected she would. He offered her a cigarette, which she took.

"Doing OK?" he asked her.

She inhaled, held it, and let it out slowly. "Yeah. No more bikinis, but yeah."

Leah was turning out to be a very useful spy; Dan had heard that Mark had tried hard with her when she got out of the hospital wing, but she seemed to have shut that door in his face.

"What about Penny?" she asked. He knew this was coming from someone, and knew that whatever he said would probably become common knowledge within a day.

There was the truth, and then there was the truth they all needed to move on together. "She's been under a bit of pressure. The stress of us lot getting put through a blender didn't help, I should imagine. She's done well getting everyone organised for the winter, though, don't you think?" he said, turning to Lexi for her turn.

"Yep. She's not, you know, planning on changing things or anything?" she asked innocently.

Dan matched her innocence. "Like what?"

"Well. We still work for you, don't we…?" she said, trailing off in uncertainty at the boundaries she was pushing.

Rumour really did spread fast, he thought. "Yes. You do. Why, did you hear that she was planning on any changes?" he challenged.

"No, no," said Lexi, "I was just checking."

Dan finished his cigarette, called his dog and went to watch the film. Luckily, Leah missed out. He settled down with his thoughts spinning, pretending to watch a film with the others.

WINTER WONDERLAND

Days rolled into weeks. Frosts came and it tried to snow a few times. Everyone was wrapped up well; the boxes of thermal sports base layers lifted from the camping store were a good buy.

Dan went with black base layers under his standard black clothes. He had got a black arctic waterproof and windproof pullover from one of their scavenging trips during the hot weather. He had dug it out and now pretty much lived in it.

Curiously, he noticed that the other Rangers had followed suit in style noir, which adorably included Leah. Her black boots had her black combat trousers tucked in, and she added about four layers of tops and fleeces topped off with a black woollen hat.

Dan had kept the beard and hair a little longer, but still the same length all over, which both Joe and Steve had adopted. Dan's bandaging had come off, exposing the straight line of delicate stitching running through the puckered skin from below his left eye and up into his hairline. Luckily, the blade had cut through his eyebrow and missed the recess of his eye socket. It itched like hell, which he knew was a good sign. Kate gave him painkillers, which he stopped taking before she recommended, much to her annoyance. He did complete the course of antibiotics which had been given to all of them. Ash had even had a course, courtesy of Sera's small medicinal stock.

He donned his own black woolly hat and went outside, pulling on his thermal gloves. The fresh, pink skin of his scarred face felt the icy stab of the cold more than the rest of him.

Ash bounded with him, fully healed long before the human casualties. Dan smoked as he walked, passing a couple of the others as they went. Ash even let the others touch him now. Dan had worked hard to have him in the house to get used to people. It was Sera's suggestion, after she had been bitten trying to stop Ash's bleeding. He was still developing and double the size he was when he was first found. He had a coarse short coat which had darkened only slightly as he matured. He glided effortlessly, loping on all fours with a casual ease that did not betray the savage speed he could employ. It was not the size of the dog that made the hits big – it was the speed it hit you at. Well, Ash was big *and* fast.

Dan walked up to the farm and back, talking with people he met as he walked. He went into Ops and Ash stalked to Leah's side, where he practically searched her for food. His snout was almost the same size as her torso.

Leah pushed the animal out of her face and produced a sheaf of papers, clearing her throat and giving Ash a Polo mint, which he crunched once and swallowed, looking expectantly for more.

"Applications," she announced. Dan picked up a plastic-wrapped pack of biscuits and poured coffee from a flask left by Steve – it was his day on duty – who was studying maps.

"Give me the highlights," he said as he sat and invited Steve to join them with a wave.

"Request for specialist item recovery," she read, then scanned her eyes along the rest of the text. "Christmas presents, actually."

Dan smiled. That kind of humanity made him happy, and he would be glad to do those runs himself, even though he bloody hated Christmas.

"A suggestion that the Rangers run a self-defence class," she said. He thought of Lexi, with her martial arts background.

"Lexi might like that." Dan was well qualified to teach also, but he didn't want another commitment on his time.

"Kyle wants to be a Ranger," she said with a smile.

Dan coughed and spat coffee as he controlled himself. "This again?" he said, annoyed. Steve gave him a questioning look and Dan explained. "Kyle is a complaining, cowardly, weak, selfish, chinless, mewling little boy who wants people to fear and respect him. He wants a gun. The answer is the same as when he asked the first time: no fucking chance."

Leah muttered "language" not quite under her breath and made a note, but Dan told her, "I'll tell him myself, though."

"Any more?" he asked.

"Request from Cedric and Maggie to run through training with people working away from the house," she said. "What to do if someone turns up, basically." Dan looked to Steve, who nodded his agreement to the silent request.

"I can throw in a bit of E&E for flavour too," Steve offered.

Dan was glad to have Steve, even with the six-inch scar across his forearm he had got for putting his eggs in Dan's basket. It was still angry and swollen, as was the stripe down his own face.

"OK, link up with Chris and find a day when the farm is covered by Logistics. Reckon you could do it within the week?" he asked.

Steve did. There were no more requests of interest, and the few more that were for Christmas presents went on the pile for a one-hit shopping trip.

He decided that there had been a long enough wait, that he was healed enough to take Joe on a trip. He went to tell Penny what he planned before finding Neil and the others he needed.

He had rounded everyone up and Ops was full. Neil, Mike, Jimmy, Ian and Joe sat to listen.

"I want to raid a police armoury." He let that hang for effect. "I need Jimmy to bring a crew under Mike and Ian's direction to use heavy machinery to breach it. Neil, there's a diesel tank in need of emptying too, so we may as well have all that while we're there," he said. "Ideas," he announced, inviting the selected group to join in.

Mike was the first to speak. "I assume we are talking stressed concrete, probably reinforced with steel?" he asked.

"I think so, and no windows," Dan replied.

"So we attack the weakest point. The lock," Mike said confidently. "Jackhammer around the door housing and a Stihl saw with a diamond-tipped blade. It won't be pretty, but it will be open."

"We've got the kit," said Neil.

"Kev can use the jackhammer; he's big enough," said Jimmy, not hiding his pride in his giant sidekick.

All in agreement, they planned to leave in an hour.

Dan and Joe went in the new Discovery, and Neil went in his Defender with Ian and Mike towing the mobile tanker with its attached pump. Jimmy and Kev borrowed Lexi's Defender, carrying a generator and the tools they needed.

Dan and Joe cleared the building, driving into the yard he had left months ago after his first burglary. There was some evidence of scavenging since he had been there last, but he highly doubted anyone could have got into the armoury. He paused to look at the now unrecognisable corpse that lay unburied in the car park where he had dumped him out of his BMW.

They cleared the building, then led Mike, Ian, Jimmy and Kev to the heavy steel door. Mike started to give instructions to the others to say what he needed, and Dan took Joe outside, leaving orders to be called when they were close to getting in.

Neil was busy pumping the diesel into his tanker, smiling at his creation again. He gave a thumbs up to them as they reappeared.

"Can you get up there?" Dan asked Joe, pointing at the roof of a police van. Joe nodded and jogged over to get the height advantage and keep watch to protect the mission. The noise started, shaking the whole building.

Dan went back inside to look for more equipment to augment their kit. He took a number of batons and six ballistic vests, as he only had two for his Rangers currently. Magazine holders and holsters from lockers went into the large bag he was carrying as the noise was replaced with the high-pitched scream of metal being cut. Ash watched him, hoping for food every time he prised open a locker.

Eventually the noise and vibration stopped, and he heard his name being shouted without urgency. He took the armful of big black kit bags he had emptied, hoping to have enough to fill them.

The doorway looked like it had exploded, with a pile of rubble pushed to one side. They had exposed the lock housing and mangled it to the point where they could force it open using the hydraulics.

Dan wasn't too happy: the racks were mostly empty. There were two Heckler & Koch G36 carbines, four Glocks, no MP5s, but there were a pair of HK416s. The carbines had the new sights which had the telescopic part you could flip to the side to use a holographic sight. They both had torch attachments; however, all the guns only had two firing selector settings: safe and semiautomatic. Not really worth the energy expended, he thought, but better than nothing.

Ammunition was stacked and spare magazines were found. He was really hoping for more. He picked up the two single-barrelled launcher guns – they basically fired a round like a solid lump of rubber. They were called AEPs, Attenuating Energy Projectiles. Non-lethal, unless you were seriously unlucky, but bloody painful.

The bags were loaded, the fuel was siphoned, and they set off home for dinner. Dan was the only one not excited; the others thought the haul was impressive.

All the new weaponry got left in the bags, ready for all the Rangers to strip them in the morning and familiarise themselves before test firing.

After dinner, Dan asked Kyle to step out with him. Kyle was very wary of Ash; he was one of the few people Ash wouldn't let touch him, which proved to Dan that his dog was a good judge of character. Dan sent Ash off into the bushes so as not to lose Kyle's attention.

"Listen, about being a Ranger," he started, glancing sideways at Kyle in the fading light. Kyle did not look happy, as if he knew where the conversation was heading. If he had a single brain cell, Dan mused, then he should. "It's not going to happen. It takes previous experience, which we all have, and we don't have the infrastructure to train someone from scratch," he said.

Kyle stopped walking. "Joe doesn't. Lexi doesn't. We don't even know if you do." His anger made him brave. Dan let the weak personal attack pass, knowing that jealousy has a strong pull.

"Joe's and Lexi's experience was enough for them to be assessed. I assessed them. They are now Rangers," he said carefully.

"WELL, ASSESS ME, THEN!" screamed Kyle. He was shaking and close to tears.

"Tell me why you want it," instructed Dan, keeping his cool.

Kyle failed the first test: he failed to control his anger. "Why should you lot get to swan around and do what you want while everyone else works? Cocky bastards. You think you're better because you've got a gun."

"Stop *now*, Kyle," Dan said coldly.

Kyle failed another test: demonstrating to Dan that he had no sense of self-preservation by carrying on. "You pick who you want. Do what you want. You're a fucking Nazi. You– " Kyle stopped, yelping in terror as Dan grabbed the front of his coat with both hands like a striking animal, pulling him close.

"Take a good look at my face, you spoiled little shit," Dan growled at him. "Does it look like it was fun? Would you have swapped places with me when I was fighting with the bastard who did this, after he took out two other people who I know for a fact would snap you without breaking a sweat? Would you even have survived this long if we hadn't taken you in?"

Kyle didn't answer; he just tried to keep himself from crying in temper.

"No, Kyle. The answer is no. You aren't capable, not only because you aren't trained, but because you only want it to show off. I have no use for you and I will never put a gun in your hand. Am I understood?" he said savagely. At the tone of Dan's voice, Ash had crept out of the dark and began to growl menacingly behind Kyle. Kyle edged away, casting a fearful look at the dog, then ran back to the house.

"Fuck it," Dan said to himself before adding, "well, that went well," aloud to Ash.

LIFE GOES ON

The next few weeks went by slowly. The old house got very cold, and gas heaters had to be used to stop people freezing. Everyone was wearing gloves and hats inside. Only two more trips were made out. One heavily protected detail visited an ambulance station now that Kate had got her medical stocks in order, with Steve, Joe and Dan going as protection while Lexi stayed behind, as she took the longest to heal from her injuries.

The other was to the closest vets, as Sera had set up a small surgery on the farm and needed more supplies. With a little more instruction from Steve, Leah was becoming very good with maps, and plotted the route easily.

Both trips were, thankfully, uneventful. Dan tried to develop some kind of routine, but he felt increasingly restless as time wore on. He wanted to be out, finding more people, but most of the group were happy to sit tight and let the cold pass. A few of them got ill, but Kate took the precaution of keeping a very close eye on them and quarantining those with viruses. She insisted that everyone take vitamin supplements with breakfast to try and avoid the colds too.

Dan received lots of sullen looks from Kyle, but he clearly lacked the conviction to make any trouble. Jack had started to spend his days either tinkering with the radio in the small hope that there was anyone on the other end, or taking trips with Pete to hunt game.

One of the cows died, and with the help of the Discovery's winch and a trailer, it was butchered and brought back to the house. They had a variation on steak every day for a month; it was tough meat, but it was food, and nobody complained.

Dan noticed that some curious pairings had started to form. Mark had given up on Lexi and had moved on to try and impress Cara. She had other ideas and seemed to have a soft spot for Matty. The effect of this was that he stayed overweight due to her cakes and extras from the kitchen.

Chris and Ana spent most days together, and in early November they moved into one of the living quarters together. Penny wanted to object, but she held her tongue at the tactful suggestions of others. Mark moved on to Eve, who seemed receptive but could barely get away from the traumatised child who clung to her legs constantly. She still hadn't spoken. Mark gave up on Eve and tried to get close to Sera, who slapped him down. Literally. Sera spent most of her free time with Kate, which most people thought nothing of, but then most people hadn't noticed what Dan had.

Lexi still tried to get time with Dan, but he tried to make it clear that it wasn't going to happen.

They had a frank conversation one evening, and he told her, "I'm responsible for keeping you safe. Think about the hospital: if I hadn't been thinking straight because we were an item, then that psycho could've killed us all."

It was a weak argument, but one that she accepted.

On the whole, people were happy. Even more so when one day a large, scruffy black cat visited the gatehouse. Ash immediately went for it, and Dan had to resort to screaming at him in German for the first time in weeks before he came away. The cat sat on the bonnet of the Discovery and hissed at the dog, who whined pitifully at being so outsmarted by a simple height advantage. Leah insisted that the cat be fed and join them. She called it Mollie, but Dan was sure it was a male and looked more of a Boris than a Mollie.

Leah would have none of it; this evil cat who taunted the dogs and scratched everyone else adored her. It would curl up on her lap in Ops and even got a bed on top of the boxed ammo, where it spent the day sleeping and being fed. If he had to stereotype the cat as a person, he was pretty sure this one had done some time in jail and wasn't to be crossed lightly.

By mid-November, Leah had compiled a long list of special items people wanted to give as Christmas presents. Dan called a council meeting – they weren't always weekly by now, as there was nothing much to report by anyone, as they were in semi-hibernation – and proposed an outing to the shopping centre where he and Lexi had found Joe and Mark. It was accepted without argument, which he found strange, and he found himself almost brokering the case against going, as nobody else objected. Unanimous agreement unsettled him. It felt like complacency, and complacency would get someone killed.

In the end, it was decided that two trips were to be made. Dan and Lexi would take one with Jimmy and Kev, and Steve and Joe would take another with Adam and Andrew. Joe knew the shopping centre well anyway, and Dan trusted Steve more than anyone but himself to keep them safe.

Leah pleaded with him to go. She was obviously getting bored. He agreed, thinking that it would do her good to get out. She must be nearly thirteen now – she had dropped her pretence of being fifteen by pure accident on the day they had found Lexi and the others – and Dan thought that she was old enough to learn some survival skills.

He started to take her out with him to exercise Ash, and after she had learned not to bounce alongside him asking questions, he started to teach her some skills.

They approached buildings he knew to be empty, starting with the gym, and he got her to practise watching the building before entering it. He gave her an empty Glock to practise weapon handling and was impressed with her. He didn't know if she was naturally good, or just naturally good at mimicking him.

He was often told that his only real skill was replicating what he saw others do, and for years took it as an insult until he saw her doing the same. He even let her fire a few rounds, but she struggled with the recoil and the noise, letting out a scream and dropping the gun once as the slide pinched her hand. He had nothing smaller to let her use, not that anything smaller would stop a cuddly toy, let alone a person.

Her pleading got through to him, and he promised to keep teaching her. In the interim, he taught her how to strip and clean all the weapons they had with the exception of the large machine gun.

The news of the shopping trips went round quickly, and others asked to come. This also went to the council, and again people were happy for "civilians" to go as long as they were adequately protected. In the end, Neil stayed home for both trips and all four Rangers accompanied a small group to the shopping centre twice.

Dan showed concern throughout the trips, as he felt that every-one was being too happy and not considering the dangers. Lexi told him he was being grumpy, which he conceded that he was. Probably.

35

Leah brought back next year's calendar for Ops, with large boxes to write things in. It was adorned with pictures of kittens.

December arrived and a wave of excitement buzzed through the cold survivors. Pete had brought in a small conifer tree one day, and Jay mounted it in a large flat slice of oak he had used as a chopping block when splitting the wood. A box of decorations was found in an office – they still had lots of unused rooms to clear out – and the place took on a happier feel. A fire burned all day in the lounge, where people had taken to congregating, as there was less work to do. The library was being well used too, probably far more so than it had ever been.

CHRISTMAS

Christmas loomed. Pete and Jack had brought down four Canada geese ready for the large meal. One of these had fallen into the lake and one of his dogs – either Tot or Dram, as Dan could never tell them apart – almost froze to death after she jumped in and towed it to the shore. Her more sensible sister took it from her on dry land and proudly presented it to their master.

The wet dog was wrapped in a blanket and cuddled in shifts by the fire until Pete put an end to her pampering and took her back to work the next day, much to her disgust.

Extra hands were recruited into the kitchen to prepare, and Penny came to Dan with a rare request of frivolity. She looked drawn and thinner in the face, but did her best to maintain her standards and presence.

"It's something of a tradition, you see," she started uncertainly. "I've checked with Andrew and he is quite certain that we have no sherry at all." She carried on with blustery explanations but he stopped her, smiling.

"Penny, if you want sherry for Christmas, I will go and get some – on one condition," he said kindly.

"Which is?" Penny asked, concerned.

"That you check there are no more Christmas requests before I leave in an hour!" he replied. She smiled and disappeared, returning thirty minutes later with a list.

Dan stood and unlocked his overstocked armoury. He took his M4 and loaded the standard five magazines he carried. As he was slowly adding the 5.56 rounds to the magazines, Leah walked in carrying the very fat Mollie, who yowled threateningly at Ash.

In response, Ash, as the savage animal he was, whimpered as he backpedalled and hid behind Dan's chair. That would explain the scratches on his nose the day before.

"Kid," Dan said to her, "put that fleabag down and help me, please."

"She isn't a fleabag!" Leah replied indignantly, but she put the cat on its perch anyway.

"Yes, he is. Sera said so, and she would know because she got scratched giving him flea medication!" he said to goad her.

"She," answered Leah flatly, bored of the same needling comments from him.

He slid a Sig to her and three magazines. "Load them with 9mm for me?" he asked nonchalantly.

Leah was understandably excited; she was being trusted with real ammunition. She deftly loaded the magazines with fifteen rounds each, then picked up the gun. He watched her carefully out of the corner of his eye, making sure she didn't accidentally shoot him. She checked the safety, seated the magazine, and then slid it home with a *click* – not slapping it in like they did in films and damaging the housing. She then held the gun to the ground and chambered a bullet.

She checked the safety again and then neatly arranged the gun and magazines on the table.

"Very good," said Dan, trying to keep it casual. "Now fetch a Glock, check the actions and load one mag," he said, pretending to concentrate on loading his own rounds.

Leah was confused, but did as she was asked. She finished at around the same time as Dan stood and went across the entrance hall to his room. It was too early for Christmas, but still. On their trip to the police station, he had brought back some ballistic body armour. As he had searched the lockers, he stumbled across the kit of what must have been the smallest policewoman ever. She couldn't have been much bigger than Leah, who was very tall for her age at nearly five and a half feet, but still very small in the torso. He had removed the police badging out of principle, and got Lou to secretly sew a pistol holster to the front cover with a double mag pouch on the lower left side. He had done this just after he had started training Leah, and hoped she would be happy with it. He had even attached a sheath holding a short four-inch knife on the front of the left shoulder, just like his own.

He donned his own armour vest and dumped the small black one on the table in front of her. She looked at it incredulously, mouth open, too scared of disappointment to believe what she saw.

Dan feigned a surprised look at her and said, "Well? Kit up, kid, we haven't got all day."

It was probably the greatest moment of her life, possibly even before everyone she knew had died.

Lexi was on duty that day, and he told her they were going out and expected to be back by nightfall. He gave her the nearby location they were going to with orders to come in force if not back when the sun was down and no radio contact had been made.

Lexi smiled at Dan's kindness and helped Leah tighten the vest over her coat. She picked up the Glock with some ceremony and pulled the topslide back slightly to see brass, just as he had taught her. Her hands were too small to do it with one hand as he did when he was showing off. She secured the weapon in the holster, which covered most of her chest, and tried her hardest not to beam with happiness.

Dan took his E&E bag, called Ash to heel, and they drove out.

Leah was at her most grown-up as they rode. Her eyes were alert, and her questions were minimal. He wasn't sure if she was actually looking or just being seen to be looking; he didn't mind either way, as she was trying.

Truth was, he could've done this short trip alone with just Ash, but it paid to prepare, and she had to get out at some point or she would die of boredom.

They found the shop they wanted after a short drive, and although Dan had personally cleared the same building three times now, he went through the full drill just as he had trained her. He mimed that she should draw her gun but not release the safety – they had discussed this in the car; she was only to take the safety off if he explicitly told her to shoot something.

He sat Ash at the door and told him to stay. The dog wasn't overly bothered, as he had done this so many times before. With their rear covered, Dan and Leah searched the small building. It was actually an old fuel station which had been turned into a Sainsbury's Local shop, and Leah moved silently as she had been taught and covered his back as he moved. He smiled to himself as she exaggerated the semi-crouch she had seen him use. The kid was a natural. Turning this into a real-life scenario where she might have to shoot a person was some way off, but if these skills were ingrained now, then she would be better than all of them when she was grown up.

He nodded to her, and she announced "CLEAR" loudly to nobody in particular, full of pride. On hearing her call, Ash trotted in, betraying the fact he knew this was just a training exercise and wasn't taking it seriously.

"Oi!" said Dan loudly, "out!" Ash turned a lazy circle and sat in the doorway of the shop where Dan told him to stay. He was the best early warning system this side of an Unmanned Aerial Vehicle. Dan produced the list and Leah got a basket. As the world had ended in early summer, there were no crackers or Christmas items lining the shelves. If it had been October when it happened, then there probably would have been, he thought sourly.

They quickly gathered what they had come for, and Dan ad libbed with bags of nuts and all the Pringles tubes he could see. They were still in date until late next year.

He led Leah back outside, where they put the basket on the back seat, called their bored sentry to jump in – he was lying down with his chin on his front paws in protest of being berated – and drove home.

Bizarrely, he had just made Leah the happiest girl ever, but that came at a price as they walked in through the main doors just as Kyle walked out. He focused on the gun strapped to the chest of a child and went pale. Dan thought he would cry or scream in rage, but he said nothing and walked out with glistening eyes.

Screw him, Dan thought. He trusted the kid more than he would ever trust Kyle. He should see if she could manage the shorter G36 soon, in the absence of finding an MP5.

Christmas Eve came, and Penny had done well organising games and entertainment. Cara had produced a seemingly endless supply of jam tarts and mince pies, and the alcohol supplies took a hit. Presents had been wrapped, and an enormous pile lay under the tree. Cards had been given as though everything were as it used to be, only this time Dan put them on the windowsill in Ops. One read: "Dear Ops and Rangers, thank you for keeping us all safe. Lots of love from the Catering department xxx."

He supposed that counted as normal now.

He felt bad that he hadn't "bought" gifts for anyone, and hadn't even thought to get a small pack of cards to give out, not that he could easily remember everyone's names. He told himself that he was busy keeping them all alive while they shopped like it was a safe activity, but in his heart, he knew it was because he was a miserable bugger.

He tried to excuse himself from the festivities on Christmas morning under the pretence of keeping watch, but nobody would let him. Even Ash was joining in, with the two cockers jumping around with him playfully.

Dan received an extensive list of presents: an indulgently costly watch with compass and altimeter, a book of jokes (obviously someone else thought he was miserable too), some items of clothing, an Action Man (someone thought they were funny), a torch mount for his Sig from Steve and a number of bottles of Scotch. Leah had got him and Ash matching bandanas with the lower half of a skull on.

42

The best present by far was something that Lexi had retrieved for Ash. Clothing for dogs was a contentious issue for Dan, but there was no doubting the brilliance of this item.

In khaki green, with a heavy grab handle and tactical loops for attachments like Dan's vest, Ash stood proudly with his own gear on. It read "K-9" on a Velcro patch on the side, and came with two pouches for him to carry a collapsible bowl and a bottle of water. Dan adjusted the straps for a better fit, and laughed with everyone else as Ash spun in circles trying to figure out with utter futility what they had done to him.

Christmas dinner was wonderful – even more so if you considered the limited cooking abilities post-apocalypse. The food kept coming, as did the cakes and the drinks.

Everyone went to bed late as the fire burned low. Dan was properly drunk for the first time since it was just him and Neil. He bid goodnight to the few left up and took his dog outside so he could smoke. He could barely stand upright, let alone still.

He rolled into his room, discarded his clothes, and collapsed naked onto the mattress where he cursed the ceiling for spinning. Just as he thought he was going to have to get up and puke, he lost consciousness.

He woke after what seemed like five minutes to light streaming in through the open curtains. It was impossibly bright, but his still-drunk brain could not compute that it had snowed heavily in the night.

He was cold, his head hurt, and as he rolled over, he realised he was not alone.

AWKWARD

She was fast asleep and either he or she, or both of them, stank of alcohol. He couldn't tell, but he cursed himself silently and racked his memory for how this had happened.

She stirred, and he didn't know whether to get dressed quietly and leave or pretend to be asleep. As he was debating this, she groaned and rolled over, snaking a soft, lazy arm over his lower back. He froze, but the hand moved down and squeezed his cheek intimately.

How the actual fuck did this happen? he thought.

He lay there in shock, one arse cheek in her hand and his mouth open, just as she opened her eyes and focused on the world. She squinted her eyes tightly at the bright light, then slowly released his flesh as it dawned on her where she was.

"Did you? Did we? Oh shit!" she said as she scrabbled the duvet up to cover her bare chest.

"What the fuck?" asked Dan in a croak, equally mortified.

It was one of the most awkward moments of his life, and combined with a murderous hangover, he wasn't having a good day already.

He looked around on the floor and grabbed some clothes. He threw them on in haste and bundled from the room, stopping in the cold hallway to put his coat, hat and boots on as his breath misted in front of his face to further cloud his vision. Ash had not taken the initiative to come with him, so he abandoned the dog to sleep in blissful ignorance of his embarrassment.

He stole outside silently as the cold hit him. His head swam. He stopped at a patch of trees about twenty metres from the front door and expelled the remaining sour contents of his stomach into the snow.

He knelt in the bushes, stomach heaving. The crunch of frozen snow underfoot made him turn, his fogged brain trying to make sense of anything and everything.

The shovel hit him hard in the right side of his head and shoulder, the blow deflecting as he flinched away from it. It sprawled him face down, choking him with a face full of dirty slush.

"Not better than me now, are you?" whined his attacker in a peevish voice, close to tears as he raised the shovel high above his head again.

~

Kyle had been waiting for him. He was going to have one last attempt at convincing Dan to try him out and see if he could shoot. He had wanted to attend Lexi's self-defence class but was too bigoted to accept instruction in fighting from a woman, regardless of the fact that Lexi was arguably one of the most capable people there.

Despite being told exactly why, he still thought he could cajole his way into being tested where he could prove himself and finally be a Somebody.

The final straw was when he saw her go into his room. He realised, as he saw Dan stagger outside, that he was wasting his breath by planning to speak to him. This man, a bully in Kyle's eyes, would never let him join his elite. Dan would never make him one of them. Just like everyone else in Kyle's life, this man was better than him and he knew it.

But not today: he had no guns, and that bastard dog of his was nowhere to be seen. He would show this man what he could do.

He picked up the shovel left by the front door to clear snow and walked behind him. He thought himself stealthy, but in truth he would never have got anywhere near the man if Dan wasn't so drunk; he simply wasn't aware of anything.

As Dan retched onto the ground, Kyle swung the shovel like a cricketer, aiming to send Dan's head clear over the boundary. The bastard turned at the last minute, making Kyle miss his face. Kyle recovered himself and started to beat the shovel down on him, over and over. He cried aloud as he did it. He cried for all the years he had been laughed at, rejected, bested, left behind and ignored while the Dans of the world got the recognition and the women. The people good at sports, the ones who had muscles – fuck all of them.

Dan spun onto his back and used his legs. He held off maybe ten or fifteen blows before a slipped footing rewarded him with a stinging blow to his right knee. He involuntarily reached for it, and took a heavy hit to the top of his head. Darkness flashed, and the pain was unbearable.

Kyle was so enraged, so consumed in his attack, that he did not see Ana and Chris coming out of the house on their way to the farm. They saw him, but it took a few seconds to realise that he was attacking a person and not venting frustrations into the snow. Ana shouted and started to run towards him as Chris took the twelve-bore shotgun from the slip on his back and fired twice in the air.

Kyle realised he had been caught. He faced a choice: stay, and this bastard would surely kill him, or run.

He ran.

Chris and Ana went to help Dan, who was covered in blood. He had taken a massive amount of damage, and combined with his hangover, he lost consciousness.

Others ran from the house, pulling on clothes as they rushed headlong into the cold. Confusion reigned, and shouts for explanations rang out. Chris handed Ana the gun and went to lift Dan up, only stopping when Kate screamed a command to leave him. She ran over and saw the injuries to Dan's head and the discarded shovel on the ground, barking orders for the stretcher and spine-board to be brought from medical immediately. She had to get him off the ground quickly to avoid hypothermia, but carefully so she didn't aggravate the likely neck injuries he had.

Penny strode from the house, her commanding voice demanding an explanation for the commotion. She saw Dan, bloodied and battered in the snow, and stopped.

"Oh dear God!" she said. "Who did this?"

Ana spoke first. "It was Kyle." She still pronounced it "Keel". "He hit him with…" She was lost for the translation, although it was obvious, and pointed to the shovel, saying "Cobok.

"We see him, and he run," she finished lamely.

Dan was brought inside strapped to the stretcher with blocks on either side of his head. Heaters were brought in and a fire lit in medical, as his body temperature had already fallen dangerously low from the short time on the wet ground. People buzzed around, asking questions until Kate roared at them all to get out.

"Anybody not medically trained is to leave right now!" she bawled as her temper frayed too far, standing square to stare down the room until they fled. Only she and Lizzie remained.

Dan was unaware of all this as he lay unresponsive on his back, dripping diluted snowmelt and blood onto the floor.

WE MUST RETAIN OUR HUMANITY

Dan was out for most of the morning. When he did come round, he could not move his head. This resulted in him fountaining acidic bile into the air for it to fall in his face. He would have choked had Kate not run over to him and tipped his entire immobile body over for the sick to go with gravity. She cleaned him up and began an in-depth top-to-toe survey where she tested his feeling all over.

No obvious spinal damage. She turned him the other way and felt down every single segment of his vertebrae, asking each time if he had pain or numbness. He didn't. She checked his skull thoroughly, looking for signs of fractures. After checking his pupil response for the fiftieth time, she finally allowed him to remove the head blocks and move around. Kate was still unhappy.

"I'm only guessing, you realise," she said testily. "You should have a full spinal X-ray or a CT preferably."

Dan tried to reassure her that he was fine, and that she was doing a great job without modern machinery. He could barely get the words out from the swollen right side of his jaw.

"Council members," he mumbled, "please."

He was soon looking up at the concerned faces of Penny, Andrew, Neil, Jimmy, Cara and Chris. Kate was still flitting around him, but she had sent Lizzie to take a break.

Dan had told a version of events which left out some embarrassingly key details. Where his consciousness ended, so Chris's story began. He learned how the cowardly bastard Kyle had run into the woods rather than face the consequences.

Kate reported that Dan was lucky, that one of the blows could easily have paralysed or killed him. Neil reported that Steve, Joe and Lexi had gone after Kyle, but as Ash was too wound up over Dan being down to go with them, they lost track of him after a mile.

Dan wanted to get his dog and his gun and hunt the bastard down. He said as much to the council, but even he had to agree he was in no state to move anywhere for a while. He left out the more creative ideas of what he could do when he caught him.

Kyle's actions had brought about the difficult question of punishment. The only one internal problem they had ever encountered had resulted in the public humiliation and ejection of Callum some months ago. That was different: that was a fight as such and not a deliberate action by the leaders of a group of people. It wasn't society punishing a crime.

Was Kyle to be banished? That held inherent dangers in that he knew where they were and what capabilities they had. He could return with others and be a serious threat to them.

Someone suggested execution, which Dan thought was a good idea at first, but the more he thought of it, the more he knew it was the wrong way to go: killing someone was one thing, but executing them for a crime was different – even if it was an attempted murder.

Neil pointed out that it was irrelevant, as Kyle was in the wind anyway and was unlikely to live long without shelter and equipment.

From what Chris said, he ran with just the clothes on his back, so would probably die of exposure before the new year.

Penny suggested that if he returned or was captured, then he should stand trial. Dan wanted to protest that he was seen by three people doing it and then ran away. No mitigation he could offer could excuse his actions, especially as he fled after. Dan held his tongue, though – as anarchical as he felt, he still believed in justice, although his beliefs were in a deeper and purer justice than the world had known before it happened.

The subject was ended under the cloud of crossing bridges when they came to them, and he was left to sleep. He wasn't sure how badly hurt he was, as the hangover symptoms seemed worse than the head injuries.

Sera brought Ash to him later that day, and the huge dog hurt him again by climbing onto the hospital bed as he had a matter of weeks before. He refused to leave and growled at Kate when she told him to get down, prompting Dan to reprimand him and send him out with Sera.

Dan would've preferred to go back to his own bed, but Kate insisted on twenty-four hours' observation, especially the way he "liked to collect concussions," she added.

He was released by lunchtime the next day and walked stiffly to the front door. He let Ash out on the way past and leaned against his truck to smoke. Steve joined him and told him of the brief hunt for Kyle, but without a dog, they were too far behind to find him.

"Pete tried with his girls, but they just put pheasants up instead," he said, laughing.

"Ash would've caught him and tore the little fucker to pieces," Dan growled, looking at the dog. Sensing he was being discussed, he cocked his head over and stared at Dan with his ears up, waiting for food or praise or both. Dan fussed his head.

"I don't fancy his chances, though," said Steve. "I've seen people die in better conditions, and he has no tradecraft at all from what I hear." Steve's eyes glazed over, deep in memory.

"Where have you gone, mate?" Dan asked kindly.

"The cockpit of a Merlin. Kosovo," he replied quietly.

Dan put a hand on the pilot's shoulder as he passed. They all had their history, and post-traumatic stress was probably the only single common denominator for them all.

Dan had his own skeletons too, just not of the frozen wasteland mass genocide type.

Steve felt instantly guilty for the lie.

True, he had seen some awful atrocities during his service in the Balkans and elsewhere, but nothing compared to the soldiers actually on the ground. In his head, he had really gone back to Snowdon years ago. A sudden storm had hit them when walking, and he had had to lead his wife and kids down before the weather became a danger to them.

Dan limped back into Ops, where Leah fixed him with a smile of relief. The mangy cat hissed at Ash from its perch: a Sainsbury's shopping basket with a prison blanket inside on top of a five-foot-tall stack of 5.56 bullets in boxes.

Ash responded with a whine of fear and frustration as he backed away from the evil thing.

Lexi blushed and looked at the floor. He wasn't in the mood, but he had to deal with this soon.

Steve walked back in and went straight past Ops, deep in thought. Dan made a show of producing his packet of cigarettes, announcing clearly without words that he was going back outside. As he had hoped, Lexi followed him.

He lit two cigarettes at once and handed her one in silence. He walked with some difficulty to the place where Kyle had attacked him.

He laughed mirthlessly; that was probably the only conceivable circumstance in which Kyle could ever have beaten him.

But he had, and it was very nearly final.

"I'll kill the bastard if I find him," she started.

"You won't, because if he's not already dead, I doubt he will last more than a couple of days," he replied tiredly. "Any idea what set him off?" he asked, subtly raising the subject.

"We didn't do anything," she blurted out, turning crimson. "I just–"

"You just what?" he asked carefully.

"I just didn't want to spend Christmas on my own," she said to the floor. "I was drunk and I just got in your bed, that's it."

He sighed. "Lex, we've been through this."

"I know," she said. "Kyle tried it on with me last night, and I was," she hesitated, searching for the right word, "unkind to him. Cruel, actually. Then he probably saw me go to your room. It's my fault."

"No, it isn't," said Dan. "It's Kyle's for being a fucking jealous prick and mine for letting the rat get the drop on me. You know I roughed him up the other day and Ash saw him off?"

Lexi's eyebrows rose.

"Yeah," said Dan, "he demanded to be a Ranger. Again."

Lexi laughed. "I bet he shit a brick when you gave Leah a Glock!"

Dan wasn't in the mood to laugh at Kyle's wounded pride; his injuries were still too sore. He started to walk back to the house.

"So, we good now?" Lexi asked after him.

"Yes," he said, not entirely convincing himself as he recalled her bare chest in his bed covered in scars she received for doing the job he gave her.

CABIN FEVER

After the excitement of Christmas and Kyle being branded an outlaw, New Year came and went without the grand celebration of previous times. Perhaps people were more pensive about the passing of time and making resolutions without sharing them with the loved ones they'd had last time around.

The mood became low, and then tempers started to fray. Suggestions were made for scavenging runs, mostly for people to get out. Neil insisted Dan take him out for petrol, as the generators had used up almost all of his stores. Dan knew he still had over three hundred litres of petrol, but humoured him anyway. Six people volunteered to come. In the end, they went on their own, travelling further afield just for the hell of it.

One of the main reasons for Dan putting a stop to the trips during winter was that the roads, without proper maintenance and gritting, were degrading fast and were treacherous in places. He had to go slowly, avoiding potholes and even subsidence at one point. They had ten jerrycans to fill and two hand pumps to do it with.

Neil removed the reservoir locks as he had done before and suggested a race to fill the first can. Dan smiled, and asked what the stakes were.

"Name your price, monsieur," Neil replied in a sleazy French accent.

"I win, you do my washing up this week," he said.

"Likewise," Neil said, offering his hand. As Dan took his own hand from the pump to shake Neil's, the older man shouted "GO" and began to pump furiously, making Dan curse and rush to try and catch up.

They couldn't call a clear winner, and sat panting and laughing together as Ash gave them both a questioning look. They finished the other cans at a more sensible pace and went to set off home. They drove for a few minutes before Neil stared ahead, leaning towards the windscreen.

He held up a pointed finger in silence, making Dan look to his right, where a pillar of black smoke was rising behind a copse of trees in the distance.

They exchanged a look, and Dan turned the Discovery towards the possibility of people. They struggled to find the source of the smoke, and when they got close to where they thought it was, they found a golf course blocking their path. They had to drive a long detour with Neil keeping an eye on the Ordnance Survey map of the area. Eventually they found a long, looping road which had housing estates branched off at intervals to the right and industrial areas to their left.

The source of the smoke was the bonnet of a crashed Ford Transit minibus, the unfortunate driver having taken advantage of the relaxed seatbelt laws of late. His shattered and twisted frame was sprawled through the broken windscreen where his upper body was starting to cook from the heat of the small fire which hadn't yet erupted to engulf the entire vehicle. Dan had seen enough in his life to know that the driver was killed on impact, and that the whole lot would be afire soon. Bags were strewn about in the back and on the ground next to the open sliding door.

"Someone survived," Dan said, pointing to the uneven tracks in the wet grass leading to the overgrown bushes separating the road from an industrial area.

Neil had not come armed, so Dan handed him his Sig as he retrieved the M4 from the cab. He whistled Ash to his heel and locked the Land Rover before setting off after the survivors of the crash. The tracks were a mess, like whoever had left them was dragging something in a hurry.

The more Dan looked at the tracks, the more concerned he grew. There were gouge marks intermittently, like whatever they were dragging was fighting back. He hadn't survived this long by being careless, so he sank to a crouch and readied his weapon as he whispered his suspicions to Neil.

The older man switched on immediately and his happy demeanour melted away to reveal his darker, more serious side. Dan made eye contact with Ash before giving him a hand signal; Ash understood and sank into a stalk as he moved silently alongside his master.

Moving carefully meant moving very slowly. It was close to five minutes before they were rewarded with a low grumble from Ash's patented early warning system. They slowly circled a building before finding a vantage point where Dan could see what was inside. It was a warehouse and looked similar to their own stores, but not organised by any standard. Crates of bottles and tins were ripped open in no particular order. He heard a male voice speaking, and what sounded like a female voice responding angrily.

He scanned the room and saw movement off to his right. He assessed what he saw and considered his options before deciding to play this one dumb. He stripped off his body armour and swapped weapons with Neil. He tucked the Sig in the back of his trousers before creeping alongside the building to where the shutter door was rolled up. He sat Ash flush to the building, so a person would have to be outside before they saw him. He made him stay with eye contact and hand signals before walking away to come to the building from the direction of the road.

He put his hands in his pockets and scuffed his feet as he walked, trying to demonstrate no threat in his body language.

"Hello?" he called as he approached the door.

The man who had been talking visibly jumped in fright and wheeled on Dan holding a gun. Dan recognised it as another Glock, and thought that this weapon had probably been sourced in the same way he had his own in the beginning.

The man held it sideways, like he was in a film. Dan felt a surge of disappointment at the low standards of this newest adversary, suspecting that he was going to have to converse with a mouth-breather; ever the post-apocalyptic snob.

"What the fuck do you want?" he asked, scared and edgy. He walked away from the woman and Dan saw her clearly for the first time. Her blonde hair was a mess, and her big eyes pleaded with him for help but burned with a mockery that said she would never lower herself to actually beg for his assistance. He made no response to her look, but focused on the man with the gun.

He advanced on Dan, still holding the gun sideways and evidently scared by the intrusion. Dan thought that if this idiot was going to walk up to him and hold the gun to his head, then this was going to be easier than he suspected. The aggressor stopped short of the threshold, about ten feet from where Dan stood with his hands up.

Dan willed him to close the gap between them and make it easier to remove him from the equation. A glance at Ash showed that he wasn't in play yet; their new enemy needed to walk forward a few more feet for the dog to surprise him.

"I said, what do you want?" said the man testily. His aggression failed to mask the panic evidently rising in him. He forced himself to sound in control, only managing to cover his fear with an excess of hostility.

"Who is it?" came another voice from inside. It wasn't the woman, as she sat and stared at Dan with almost a sense of amusement at the turn of events.

That complicated things; there was at least one other in there and he had no clue yet if they were armed as well.

"Whoa, mate!" said Dan, intentionally attempting to mimic a local accent in an attempt to dumb down. "Was that you that had a crash back there?" he said, stalling for time.

"No, someone else. We helped them," he said uneasily.

"They ran us off the road and dragged me here," the woman started to shout indignantly before another man stepped into view and slapped her hard across the head, messing her hair up further and receiving a murderous look in response. Dan involuntarily stepped forward, but the man with the gun pointed it in his face.

"Not one more step; she's ours. Get lost," he said nervously, waving the end of the barrel at Dan. He could barely keep the gun still. Dan now had to take out two in quick succession before the woman got hurt. Simply leaving was not an option for him now. He stepped backwards and stared at the man.

"What are you going to do? I bet you don't know, do you? Look at you, you're a joke," Dan said softly as he walked backwards, goading him.

The man reacted as he was supposed to: with his masculinity affronted, he stepped forwards to close the gap with Dan and threaten him again, to be close enough to see his fear.

As the hand holding the gun advanced into the daylight, Dan saw Ash tilt his head to marvel at the new toy he was being presented with. A second later, Ash launched, taking the arm and the body attached to it. The force of the impact and the momentum of the dog was sufficient to yank the man's neck painfully as he was taken to the ground. Dan stepped to the side, simultaneously drawing the Sig from behind his back.

Dan walked past Ash ripping at the man without taking his eyes off the second target; he had to trust the dog to do his job, as speed was paramount. Untrained people took triple the time to react, and he capitalised on that.

As the second man saw what was happening, he reached out and grabbed the woman, reacting far quicker than Dan expected.

Too late for Dan to strike, he held a knife to her throat and looked terrified and desperate, whereas the woman showed a marked contrast with her obvious calmness. The man with the knife had the same twitchiness as his companion, who still screamed in Ash's teeth.

"Get your dog off him!" he bellowed fearfully, pressing the knife into the flesh above the woman's collarbone.

"No. Let her go and I'll call my dog back," Dan said in a low monotone. Give the appearance of calm and their panic would rise.

"NO!" he snapped in retort over the noise of snarling and pained screams, trembling.

Dan thought that this man was likely to cut her deeply by pure accident in his state of panic. He glanced at the woman, still pointing the Sig at the man holding her.

"What's your name?" he asked her in the same low voice.

"Marie," she said through gritted teeth. "Lovely to meet you, but please get this fucking arsehole off me." Sarcasm in the face of adversity. She got more attractive by the second.

"Marie, I'm very sorry," he said. The look of confusion on her face was replaced by open-mouthed, horrified shock when Dan fired a single round.

The desperate man's biggest mistake was that he had let Dan get to within ten feet as he spoke, so close that he could not miss. The bullet entered his face just under the nose, tearing a ragged hole through his top lip, shattering the teeth behind before blowing the brainstem out. The hand holding the knife had no chance to cut her accidentally, as it was instantly lifeless without the possibility of any nerve receiving a signal from the brain.

Marie stood still with her mouth open, and blood splattered on her face as her captor fell to the floor, utterly lifeless. Dan heard the percussive cough of a suppressed weapon firing outside, and he ran to find Neil had fired at, and killed, a ragged-haired woman running at Ash with an axe. Dan thanked him, and called Ash away from the dead man he was still tearing at.

"Good boy, leave it," he said. Ash trotted to his side without reluctance, happy with the praise. His muzzle, face and chest were soaked red with the man's blood. He walked back inside, where he found Marie wiping the gore from her face in horror. Dan went to speak to her, but was met with a snarl.

"In my hair? Thanks!" she said, then took a breath and steadied herself. "No, seriously. Thanks," she said, and raised herself on tiptoes to kiss his cheek, transferring a small amount of brain matter to his face.

She walked to a door and opened it, revealing another woman and a man who was groggy with a lump on his head. The woman was much shorter and heavier than Marie; she was Asian, had long dark hair and an almond-shaped eyes. She saw the spreading puddle of dark red blood on the ground and looked instantly unwell, hugging Marie tightly. In contrast, Marie seemed to be unfazed by their ordeal.

The man was barely conscious and couldn't quite understand what was happening. Dan checked him out and hoped it would pass, as he could detect no serious trauma. With help, he laid him on a heavy plastic sheet as a makeshift stretcher.

He retrieved the Glock and found no other weapons of use. They left the bodies where they were and spirited the women outside, where he took back his kit from Neil. He used a bottle of water from inside to wash the blood from Ash's face, fearing that it painted him in a less than ideal light.

Marie and the other woman, Selina, told them that they were in a minibus with their friend, Anthony, when something big hit the windscreen and they crashed. They were brought here by the now deceased occupants of the warehouse and told they were staying with them now. They disagreed on that point, whereby Selina was locked in a cupboard with the man injured in the crash.

"Then you showed up with your wolf and shot the nice man I was talking to," said Marie.

Dan couldn't get a bead on her at all; she looked delicate, and if forced to guess, he would have said she was the "hide in a corner and cry" type as opposed to the "make jokes about seeing someone shot in the face twelve inches away" type. She fixed him with a smile to show she was joking, and he felt himself colouring up. He liked her. She disarmed him completely and made him feel like an awkward boy.

"I assume you two live somewhere near here?" Selina asked, changing the subject.

"We have our own manor house and grounds," said Neil pompously. He pronounced grounds as "grinds", making Dan smile. He'd used the very same impression when they first met.

"And there are almost forty of us," Dan added. That got a response from the two, who exchanged a look.

Selina asked, "All immune?"

"I assume so; none of us got sick when it happened," he said, then changed the subject again as they walked to the Land Rover.

"Where did you come from?" Dan asked.

"Racist," said Selina mockingly. "My family's from Bolton and I moved down for university." Neil laughed at her sense of humour.

"No…" Dan stuttered. "I meant…"

"We know what you meant, silly sally," said Marie. "We had to leave the city because supplies were running out and the smell was awful. There were also a lot more people like them back there making it unsafe to stay," she added.

"So, what do you ladies do?" asked Neil politely as he called a stop to readjust his grip on the makeshift stretcher.

"Selina's a madam in one of Europe's most prestigious brothels and I'm an award-winning pole dancer," Marie said, without even a hint of frivolity.

Both men were taken aback by this, and both felt instantly foolish when the women started to laugh simultaneously.

Marie sighed. "I am – was – a Detective Sergeant in the city's Major Investigation Team." She let that hang and noticed a close scrutiny from Dan. "He is some kind or architect, but to be honest I switched off whenever he spoke about work," she finished. "He" was called Paul, and was looking a little green from the concussion.

"Well, I'm a pharmacist… Student," said Selina, feeling totally upstaged by Marie, who was still locked in a staring match with Dan. "Shall we give you three a little time alone?" she asked them politely.

Dan snapped out of his trance to see that his bloodstained dog stared at Marie as intently as he had been doing, one lip curled up in a wonky smile.

LOVED OR UNDERSTOOD?

Dan and Neil drove their new additions back in awkward silence. Dan kept stealing glances at Marie in the rearview mirror, which he caught Neil noticing.

They spoke freely of their experiences in the last few months, of how people in the city who had survived the virus – it was a virus in Selina's opinion – had simply died of a lack of basic skills such as the ability to find water when their taps ran dry and the local shop was looted.

Twice before, they had encountered hostile groups who wanted to take rather than build. They were the last of five people originally in the group; one died on the bonnet of their minibus and the other had killed himself about two weeks after he found them. Marie said that this was very selfish of him, as they had to clean it up.

The Glock was originally hers, taken on a whim from the holster of a dead colleague before she gave up and left work for the last time, but she was the first to admit that she had never fired one and hadn't a clue how they worked; she had devoted her life to catching the people who used them on others.

Paul was deposited immediately into the care of Kate, who made loud noises about people plaguing her with serious head injuries. Marie and Selina were given the guided tour of the house by Dan. He didn't want to seem eager, but he couldn't bear to part with Marie so soon; there was something intriguing – no, enchanting – about her.

He took off his kit in Ops and allowed Leah to clean the M4 and two pistols; his own weapons were dirty through firing, and the Glock through neglect. Leah was keen to show off, and Steve was there to keep an eye on her and make sure nobody was killed by a stray bullet ricocheting around the office by accident. Selina made a comment about child soldiers which went ignored.

He was as thorough as he could have been with the tour, introducing everyone he could remember the name of, and offered to show them the farms and garden to extend the time.

"No thanks," said Marie. "I'd love a cup of tea and a shower, though."

Dan said he couldn't help with the shower, and then turned red as his courage abandoned him entirely.

Penny gladly took them away from him and explained how the water was heated in the bathrooms for washing. They were taken to their clothing store, or "Primark" as it had been dubbed.

Lexi returned from the gym where she had been teaching a chilly self-defence class and heard of the new arrivals. She poked her head into medical and shrieked.

"Paul!" she squealed, running to his bed and landing on him. A barrage of questions followed, none of which he could answer, as he was still barely conscious. Kate ejected her from the wing and she excitedly grilled Dan for answers.

"We rescued three from the local cast of *Deliverance*," he said. "I know nothing more about the bloke."

"I do!" she said, almost hyperactively. "He's an instructor at my club! He's amazing!"

Dan could not say he was put out to hear that she had interest in another man.

"Just wait until he's better!" she said. "He'll be able to teach everyone better than I can!" And with that, she bounced from Ops.

Dan and Steve exchanged looks of surprise. Lexi had a crush on the man, and luckily he was still alive.

At dinner, the new arrivals – bar Paul, who was in medical with Lexi waiting on him – were greeted by Penny. They were told to relax for the night and tomorrow they would be found a role to play.

For Selina, that was purely academic: as someone with pharmaceutical knowledge, Kate had laid a very strong claim to her as a medical assistant.

Marie was a different matter. Dan wanted her close, purely for selfish personal reasons, but she had no interest and no skill with firearms. She had other necessary requirements for the Rangers, but he had to find a way to keep her with his unit where he held sway.

She had not made a big deal of her skills, saying, in a self-effacing manner, that she probably had very little to offer. Dan thought of expanding the Ops role to justify having both Marie and Leah there.

Because the group's numbers had grown so much that he could not keep up, Dan could not get close enough to Marie after dinner to capitalise her time without looking obvious. He gave up and went outside to smoke.

To his surprise, Marie also came outside and lit a cigarette. She saw him and raised a conspiratorial eyebrow. "Dying breed," she said solemnly. "Very few of us antisocial smokers left in the world now."

It seemed to be a well-rehearsed "break the ice" smoking conversation. He didn't know what to say. All of his moody swagger deserted him when she spoke.

"Have you thought of joining the Ops department?" he asked in the absence of anything better to say.

"Can't say, to be honest. Not sure I'd be much use to you gunslingers. I'm more used to pointing your type in the direction of baddies and saying 'fetch'."

Her smile took all the insult out of her words.

He tried to reason with her, saying, "It's not about gunslinging – it's about tactical planning more than anything."

She said nothing, so he pressed his advantage.

"Fancy a drink?" he offered.

"Long day," she replied flatly. "I'll probably just get to bed."

Dan accepted this as chivalrously as he could, but reflected that he probably still seemed like a jilted boy as he walked inside, calling Ash after him. He stripped off his coat as he stood in his room, hoping for another glance of the captivating woman who was not in the slightest bit impressed with him. He gave up and went to bed.

REVENGE

"Revenge is an act you want to commit when you are powerless, and because you are powerless," said Billy magnanimously.

Kyle thought that he couldn't give a single shit for the theory; he just wanted to hurt Dan. Badly.

He had run across country for as long as he could remember, terrified of that dog chasing him down and ripping his flesh like he had heard it did during the hospital fiasco.

He had run for hours with no clear direction or purpose.

As it got dark, he had no idea where he was, but he saw light from a fire and he heard voices. He ran towards it, and as he burst through the trees and into their camp, he collapsed with exhaustion.

The group seemed startled to see him emerge into their camp. They looked to Billy, who seemed to be calling every shot.

Now he sat, wrapped warmly and given food and alcohol, and listened.

"Relax, Kyle," said Billy with a smile. "You are amongst friends now."

Kyle was petty and selfish, but he wasn't entirely stupid. He was a little worried about who these men were and what they did to people they found.

"What's brought you to us, then?" said Billy.

He was unsure whether to tell the truth at first, but his anger at how he felt he had been mistreated was very raw. Tears stung at his eyes as he realised what he had done, blaming anyone but himself. He told them about the house, about Dan and the Rangers, about how they strutted around with their machine guns while others had to work for their food. Billy lapped it all up, making the right noises and pulling sympathetic faces when Kyle's indignation reached its height.

"I think we can help you, Kyle," he said, smiling a dangerous smile.

Kyle would have his revenge on Dan and his smug bastards.

SITE THREE

She had to admit that things were getting tiresome. There was only emergency-generator power for the lighting and air recirculation, and this was run on a huge underground fuel tank. The systems were augmented by external solar panels, but these weren't enough to rely on alone, especially as they needed cleaning and were probably still covered in leaves.

The generator was used to top up the batteries, and every day the power levels dropped slightly lower than the day before. One of the staff reckoned it would only last another month or so, and then they would be forced to go topside.

Months ago, the order had come for the cabinet to lock down, as an epidemic was feared. There was a query regarding biological warfare, which nobody had a definitive answer to.

They had watched for two days how the country fell apart. Hospitals were inundated at first, then totally overwhelmed when people started to die. Looting started as soon as the bounds of social cohesion began to fray, which surprised nobody. Quickly, even the looters started to get sick and die. By the time the external power grid failed and severed their link to the cameras outside of their immediate control, there was nobody moving.

Four senior politicians had got through the screening process, which was basically that anybody who had the slightest raise in body temperature was deftly diverted to another room which did not lead to the bunker. With those politicians had come some key senior military commanders and their bag carriers, along with members of research staff who had been in place for some time, judging by their pale complexions. Add to this the maintenance staff and a handful of police officers assigned to escort and protect the politicians, and there were thirty-six souls locked underground.

There had been thirty-seven, but one man was determined to open the sealed entrance and condemn them all in the hope that his family were still alive. One of the police officers had abruptly ended negotiations with the enraged man using a gun.

Now it seemed, after months of living underground, there was no rescue coming and no contact from the outside world either. Satellite phones, secure digital hard line networks, Internet, radios – all had gone quiet weeks ago. People started to say that this was a global event, and speculation ran wild.

Eleven similar locations on the UK mainland had been activated simultaneously, and communications between four others had been established. Three of those showed signs of outbreak within twelve hours of lockdown, and all contact was lost shortly after. The safe assumption was that they had all died.

Contact only remained with one other bunker – site one – over five hundred miles away in Scotland. It was in a very remote location intentionally, and was the secret base of virology where bioweapons were tested and constant theoretical war games were played.

A modern-day plague was the new nuclear option, it seemed. Even better, actually, as it was deniable. The virology lab held synthesised accelerated samples of just about everything that could kill a person, and then tried to find ways of juicing its lethality to biblical proportions. Information security protocols were adhered to in the first few weeks, but as it started to dawn on everyone that this was very real, so the story began to unfold.

From what the scientists had seen, this was a form of influenza, based on their observations on camera. It had an unbelievably fast gestation period and was lethal within forty-eight hours. Exact cause of death was unknown, as no test subjects were available to be autopsied, but the best guess would be fever and heart failure. They swore it wasn't one of theirs, and voiced suspicions that if it was a bioweapon attack, then it would probably be airborne and most definitely Chinese.

There were some in the bunker with various religious beliefs. Some of these hypothesised the coming of the end of days, which led to counterarguments and eventually a number of heated fights which had to be split up more than once.

An ageing lieutenant colonel with an impressive shock of white hair and a dazzling array of medals was all for their immediate departure; he planned to lead them all to a nearby barracks where they would be equipped as soldiers and he would lead them onwards.

Most people thought the man unstable, and it was rumoured that the last time he had seen active service was before most of them were born.

Their decision was made for them at the end of February, when the generator began to splutter and finally gave out. This year's resolution: don't die of suffocation in a hole in the ground.

BACK ON THE HORSE

February ended and the weather improved slightly. A flurry of activity began on the farms and gardens: seeds were planted, animals were moved around and Chris spoke of his plans to introduce the young bull to their small herd of cows.

All departments loaned extra bodies to help, and some renewed purpose infected the group. Dan decided to start pushing the fitness and skills of his Rangers, and had them in the gym three times a week where he ran them until they sweated, then made them lift weights and finish with a session on the mats where they drilled over and over with close-quarters scenarios. Leah kept up as much as she could and paid close attention to the lessons in weapon retention. She had also been training with Lexi and was starting to develop some muscle.

Twice Dan had overtly tried to get Marie to be part of Ops, and both times she flatly refused him. He raised good points with her skills of planning and organising being an asset, but her mind was made up. He had even approached Penny about it, but she was firmly on Marie's side.

Marie felt her professional experience was of no value yet: there weren't enough people to police and nothing to investigate. She had decided to use her education in a more practical setting, and after some discussion, she became the group's first mental health professional. She had a degree in psychology, and through her work had been trained as a counsellor. She had also studied art and offered to run a drawing class for anyone interested.

She was allocated a room, furniture needs were met, and the rules of confidentiality firmly set. Similar to the medical records being established, Marie met each member of the group in turn, taking nearly two weeks, and discussed how they were coping. Nearly half of the group booked a return visit.

Dan grudgingly attended, and he was as closed off about his past as he always was, but felt tempted to book a follow-up session just so he could spend more time with her. She fascinated him, but he couldn't get close to her without looking like a lost puppy. He tried to push her from his mind; he had a lot to plan for with scouting trips and scavenging runs set to start again soon.

Lexi had fussed over Paul, who was very groggy for the first week. Kate, using complex medical terminology, had declared him badly concussed with a raft of soft-tissue injuries from the crash, and watched him like a hawk.

"What's a subdural haematoma?" Leah whispered to Dan as Kate spoke.

"It's a lump on the head," Dan answered in a stage whisper to annoy the paramedic, receiving a cold stare from Kate in reward.

Paul insisted that he felt better and was released. The subject of his employment was raised in a council meeting, and Neil asked to talk to him with Mike to see if his architectural knowledge was of use to them.

It turned out it was: not only was he an architect but he also site-managed and had built a few commercial properties. He knew a little about scaffolding, and was instantly hired. He also, being a bit of a gym nut and heralded as a ninja according to Lexi, agreed to take over the running of the fitness and self-defence programmes.

Interdepartmental requirements had been drawn up, and a long list of supplies was needed. Scaffolding and building tools were requested for engineering, equipment and feed for the farm, and food and water for stores, as their supplies had been depleted over winter. Sera needed veterinary supplies and equipment for the horses. Kate needed medical supplies and an abundance of suturing kits, she joked. Dan raised a self-conscious hand to the neat zip marks on his face. Clothes were required, as was all the fuel they could find to keep their vehicles and generators running.

All of these requirements had to be assessed, prioritised and re-searched for the appropriate site. These sites then had to be checked by the Rangers and declared a yes or no, and a decision made on if the teams should be escorted. Dan took a long list of notes and decided to call his whole team in the next morning for an admin day and to lay down new standard operating procedures.

Neil, Mike, Carl, Ian, Adam and Paul set to work planning how the solar panel project would work and wrote endless lists of require-ments, including every vehicle battery from the larger vehicles that could be found. Jack was recruited to the engineering team for his haulage knowledge.

Andrew worked with Jimmy to prioritise the required supplies, and woke Liam from his bored hibernation. Everyone pretended not to know that he and Andrew disappeared during "generator time" to play on an old Xbox in a small room they had sequestered.

Under Chris's leadership, the farms and gardens were starting to flourish. He knew what they needed and where it could be found.

Dan decided to start the site recces as soon as possible, discussing new operating procedures as his team worked.

"Who is still happy to go out alone?" he asked them.

They all were, despite the events of last year. He was thinking of doubling up on all trips, which met some resistance from the other three Rangers. It was argued that it would put too much demand on them; maintaining a permanent guard and potentially running two trips a day would be too exhausting. He had the final say, and he was tempted to demand slower progress to make sure they always had backup. He felt that he was being overprotective, and when the realisation that he was giving advice he wouldn't take hit him, he relented.

"If a site looks dodgy, though, we send at least two to run protection," he declared as Mollie jumped onto the table and walked over their maps and notes with utter disdain.

"Leah, do you need to do some target practice?" he asked in a light tone. She smiled widely and nodded.

"Good. Shoot that bloody fleabag, please," he said, making the others laugh. Leah was annoyed at him for using her as a joke prop again and picked up the evil cat lovingly. It sat on her lap, kneading her legs with its paws and shot Dan a stare of pure loathing and superiority. He would set Ash on that thing happily, only he couldn't be sure of the outcome. If only the cat could be trained, they could pack the guns away permanently.

A prioritised list of sites and supplies was produced, and Dan deployed all four of them one morning with Neil taking over the guard.

Steve was sent to a large supermarket with Jimmy riding as observer, Lexi to the big B&Q they had checked once before with Mike, Joe to an agricultural wholesaler with Chris, and Dan went to a smaller outpatient hospital, taking only Ash, as he knew what he was looking for. They all had two or three other secondary sites which would be on the return trip, all mapped out by Leah with Steve's help.

If any of them didn't return, then the others would retrace their steps in the morning. The rest didn't need explaining; they had all been coached in escape and evasion by Steve, and all of them knew what to do. At least, Dan hoped they would.

Leah asked to go with him, but he asked her to stay and compile the reports, promising her a trip soon. Even the evident disappointment on her face could not dissuade him.

Dan reached his target by mid-morning, carefully circling the building on foot with Ash at his side. No sign of anyone, but the hospital had clearly been looted some time ago. The smell of the dead was different now – not the gut-churning stench of rotting bodies but instead the musty smell from the drying corpses which had frozen and thawed repeatedly over the winter to be twisted into grotesque poses. He thought it was best not to look at them much.

The looting appeared to have been done in haste and destructively. Dan was appalled at the unprofessionalism he saw until discovering that the only medication that seemed to have been taken was from a locked metal cabinet which had contained a dark green liquid.

Methadone. Typical that out of the world's remaining population, at least one heroin addict would have survived. The other medicines and equipment seemed mostly intact, so he made a more thorough check of the building before returning to his Discovery. He smoked as he wrote notes on the site: access point, hazards, location of supplies, et cetera.

He started on his long return route with, he guessed, five hours of daylight left. Twice more he stopped as he found the addresses of another ambulance outstation and a veterinary practice which specialised in large-animal care. Both buildings were intact, and there was no sign of danger in the areas. Dan's last stop took him past home to a motorway service station to the south.

There, he found a multitude of lorries, all waiting under the watchful eyes of dead drivers for their CB radios and large batteries to be plucked from them. On his notes, he recommended checking what the cargo was before stripping them in case they found twenty tonnes of something really useful already gift-wrapped.

He returned late afternoon and sat with Leah, who had poured him coffee. He gave his reports as instructed by the domineering almost-teenager, who he noted had donned her vest with its empty holster in honour of being the senior member of Ops on site all day. He recommended an escorted trip with Kate and Sera riding with him. One crew from logistics with a small lorry should do it. He congratulated Leah on the route, and suggested the recovery operation went the same way. Hospital first, then pick up another ambulance for Kate to drive and empty their supplies, then to the vets for Sera to pick up what she wanted.

The lorry park was a good bet, but he wanted a separate trip for that with Jack and Ian along as well as two Rangers and all the logistics crews.

Steve returned with a boot full of choice items and Jimmy ready to lead the way; there were no issues with the supermarket.

Lexi returned with Mike, who was happy that the tools they would need were readily available, and had found a well-stocked scaffolding yard on their way back, but couldn't get the loaded lorry started to bring it back.

Joe walked back in, limping and carrying a box. Chris followed as Joe deposited the box on the table. It contained three very small bundles of black fur; the story was not a happy one. They found the wholesalers with ease, and the stores there were worth going back for. As they searched through, Joe was attacked by a desperately wild collie. She was filthy and bone thin, and after she had bitten clean through Joe's trousers and taken a chunk from his calf, he shot her.

Only afterwards did Joe and Chris hear the tiny sounds the surviving puppies made after their mother had attacked the intruders to protect them. Joe felt terrible and was close to tears. Chris was far more pragmatic about it and judged that neither she nor the puppies would probably have lived through to spring. He shared that he had had to shoot one of his own dogs once, as it turned savage without warning and started killing sheep. Sera agreed with Chris's prognosis, declaring the puppies very malnourished and saying that she would be surprised if any of them lived a week.

Joe was marched into medical, where Kate set about him. Dan looked out of the window, guessing there was probably an hour of light left. He told Leah to grab Lexi's sidearm and her own emergency bag. She flew from the chair and was ready in seconds.

He pushed the Land Rover down now familiar roads, eager to be back by dark, especially as he hadn't thought to bring the night-vision goggles. They reached the small shop they had visited before, as Dan remembered seeing what they needed there. He let Leah do a quick sweep of the building – never miss an opportunity for training –

before he grabbed baby bottles and tubs of milk powder. He ended up throwing almost all of it into a bag before driving back.

It wasn't ideal, Sera thought, but it would at least give them a chance of survival.

SPRING IS IN THE AIR

Leah interviewed the three new joiners. They knew of lots of interesting things in the city, but the general consensus from all three was that the city was a bad place to visit. Marie described the place as being plagued by pirates.

What wasn't spoiled or looted was prey to roving gangs of people who wouldn't exactly be welcome in their new society. These reports were put to Dan, who decided categorically to avoid the larger population centres and stick to the more rural areas which had served them well so far. He explained this to the council and found no disagreement.

The run to the lorry park was made first. Dan wanted to lead, as always, but Steve stepped in to softly persuade him that he would go with Lexi.

They were gone from dawn 'til dusk and returned full of excitement. They had found countless trailers full of useful supplies and recovered an entire truck full of batteries. They had finally got two articulated lorries started and brought back hundreds of bottles of water in one, and another full of tinned food.

That put the trip to the supermarket on the back burner. They had encountered no problems, and Dan grudgingly left Steve in charge of the next four days of recovery runs there; they had to dump the emptied trailers nearby, as there simply wasn't room for them at the house.

Andrew was busy with all the available bodies, unloading and sorting the new loot as quickly as possible so that they could get going by the following dawn. After four days, they were exhausted, and Dan declared them officially stood down until Monday; they couldn't afford a crash through tiredness.

The next day, Dan took Adam and Jay with Sera and Kate to clear the hospital and vet's surgery.

The weekend passed without incident, and lorry park operations resumed on Monday. Jack argued to bring back a portacabin for additional storage space, which was supported. Neil also went with them, to siphon another tanker of diesel from the large tanks of the lorries.

They set the portacabin up at the side of the loading bay to their stores, and Carl began to stack and wire the lorry batteries together. It was one of those moments where having someone not qualified watching slows a professional down significantly, but it was insisted upon that he show Mike what he was doing and why. Surge protectors and other such complicated matters were discussed, all of which sailed over Dan's head – plugs, fuses and bulbs were the extent of his electrical knowledge.

By the time he returned with a lorry full of medical and veterinary supplies, another stocked ambulance – this one being a special weather one, miraculously a Land Rover Defender – and another 4x4 from the veterinary practice, the battery bank was wired and weatherproof. Leah rode shotgun for him, taking her role ever so seriously. They drove in alert silence with Ash nosing his now huge head between the seats so it seemed that all three played I spy.

The scaffolding trip wasn't a priority, as the weather wasn't yet good enough for the project, and the abundance of supplies from the lorry park was taking most personnel off site for days. Dan accepted the back seat on that detail and rotated the other three Rangers to go in pairs as the full logistics and engineering teams went out for another week.

By mid-March, they had accrued more supplies than they could actually store, and Andrew began to backfill empty barns on the gardens and farm with the sturdier food supplies. Every day, the teams went out to return with new fully laden trailers which were hastily unloaded by a kind of all-hands approach. The next morning, they would eat a large breakfast and set off again, with the group's former professional drivers putting in more hours behind the wheel than they used to.

March ended, and so did the runs to the lorry park, as they had scavenged all that they could. Pallets were added to the battery bank and another layer of lorry batteries added and wired in. Dan was sure it wouldn't pass a health and safety inspection, but as long as any fire there didn't threaten the house, then he was OK with it. Carl assured him that it was far enough away, but still added a lot of foam and CO_2 extinguishers to the shopping list.

Dan checked the Ops calendar in early April, seeing a curious marking on the following Thursday. It had hearts and stars on it, and the number thirteen.

It was Leah's thirteenth birthday.

BAD PARENTING 101

What to get a newly minted, bona fide teenager on her first post-apocalyptic birthday?

Dan had an idea, and frankly couldn't give a toss if nobody agreed.

She had earned her keep in Ops; she'd put in the boring work, studied the maps and learned everything from scratch. She could clean and dismantle weapons better than all but three of the group and had proven herself enough to be given lessons on handling the Glock. Now, if she were to take her first adult step into Dan's new trade, she would need to send something a little heavier towards the enemies of the group.

All four M4s were in use, which left the HK416s and the G36Cs. The 416 was essentially the same weapon as the M4, and in his opinion too long for her to handle easily. The G36C was shorter and only weighed a shade under four kilos. He stripped one down and checked it. It was spotless, as Leah had cleaned it under his instruction.

He had never really liked the weapon but hoped it would fit her nicely. He secretly had Lou prepare a scavenged harness from the surplus shop to hold a Glock, two spare mags and another pouch to take two mags for the G36.

He decided that it was sensible to let Steve take her for the next element of training, as he liked the sassy little girl too much to be objective if she wasn't ready yet. Still, he wanted to be the one to give her the present.

To make it less of a military-style present, he also scavenged a laptop, an iPod and lots of chart CDs he hoped she liked, and spent three entire evenings' worth of electricity time copying them onto the iPod.

He only told Penny, Lexi and Cara, and between them they planned a surprise party. He told the party committee what he planned to give her, having prepared his arguments in advance. There was some resistance to begin with, but it was Leah's wish to be trained in this field. Others reasoned that she should still learn other skills, which Dan didn't object to at all.

Whispers had gone round and plans made. Every department head decided to get her something, and one afternoon Dan and Lexi led some others on a small shopping trip to get the items on the lists.

Looting for survival was an unremarkable activity nowadays, but looting for presents and wrapping paper felt strange, like the excitement of Christmas again.

A sticky suggestion came from Kate, who raised a parallel with Leah's chosen career path and the child soldiers of African civil wars. It was done carefully to avoid insult, but made Dan pause: if an eight-year-old kid could use an AK47, then he was sure Leah could manage the G36.

Having realised that he had completely missed the point of the comment, he drifted back from his thoughts in time for the suggestion that she be given mandatory weekly counselling sessions to mentally prepare her. He thought this a great idea.

"Agreed. I'll speak to Marie about it," he said too quickly. A smirk showed on a few faces, and his further attempt to explain just left him in a deeper hole. He gave up and outlined his plan. "Leah's training will be thorough, but I have no intention of deploying her alone as a resource yet," he said as professionally as he could to recover some poise. "She must be a skilled all-rounder before that happens in the future, which includes driving and survival skills."

They all agreed; Penny visibly relaxed when she realised that Leah wasn't to be handed a gun and sent out into the remains of the world.

"I'm trying to future-proof our survival here," he said tiredly. "Who is to say how long I'll be fit to do my role? Leah will effectively be coached to replace me when she's old enough or I'm too old."

That surprised a couple of them, as they clearly hadn't thought past this generation.

"On that note," started Chris, "we could do with more people and some youngsters to start training in a similar way. I know Pete needs an apprentice."

Murmurs of agreement went round the table, and the plans for the new apprenticeships were born.

Dan's attempts to spend time with Marie were unsuccessful, to describe it mildly. She was always ahead of him, and whenever he made a clumsy suggestion, she cut him off.

He decided to be brief and businesslike instead of playing the supplicant fidgeting with his hat.

He found her room and knocked.

"Come in," she said from inside. He did, and found her with a large towel wrapped around her, and wet hair. They both had a moment of awkwardness, which she turned into his discomfort entirely by asking him what he wanted as she sat on her bed and smiled at him.

He explained briefly, stuttering his way through before he left. Crashed and burned again.

HAPPY BIRTHDAY! I GOT YOU A GUN

The morning of Leah's birthday came, and she still hadn't said anything. The day started as normal, with the morning activity causing the flow of people to congregate in the dining hall.

Leah shuffled in, groggy as always, and stopped in suspicious surprise as everyone was looking at her.

"Happy birthday!" Penny said in her singsong assembly voice.

Everyone chorused in with the same and Leah turned crimson, looking like she might cry.

Ops presented her with the laptop, and Neil gave the iPod and speaker dock from engineering, which made her squeal with delight. Cara uncovered an array of her favourite foods while Penny gave her a leather-bound diary. Chris, on behalf of the farms, gave her a set of boots like Dan's which would have cost over two hundred pounds last year. Medical, via Kate, gave her a compact field medical kit and promised her the training to use it. Next, Lou got a nod from Dan and she laid a heavy package in front of Leah. She tore at the wrapping as politely as she could, then froze.

It was her tactical vest, lifted in silence as she slept and painstakingly transformed under torchlight by Lou. She ran her hands over it and rested them on the pouches for the larger magazines. She looked at her mentor, who nodded and told her that her training was kicking up a gear.

What a terrible world, he thought, that a teenage girl was so excited to be given such things. Still, he was happy that she was happy, and oddly proud of her.

She didn't know what to do first. She ate mostly pastries for breakfast, then dressed in black combats and her new boots before bouncing back downstairs, pulling on her winter coat, which was similar to Dan's.

The weather was definitely improving with longer daylight hours, and nobody was still wearing the base layers which had been so popular over the worst of the weather. There were still some frosts, but spring felt imminent.

"You do know you've got the day off, don't you?" Dan asked as she walked into Ops.

She looked instantly deflated. "Do I get to choose what to do today?"

"OK, I'll rephrase that. You can do what you like today," he replied.

"I'd like to learn to shoot, then," she said.

Dan nodded agreement and unlocked the armoury, selecting the G36s and four magazines. They loaded them as Dan began again from the beginning about the rules for holding a firearm, this time including her mandatory counselling sessions and that her regime would be dictated by Steve.

"Aren't you teaching me?" she asked.

He thought about how to respond and tell her that he was too fond of her to be objective, in the end settling on, "Steve will be better at it and I have lots of things to do. I will be assessing you anyway."

She seemed happy enough with that, and they went for some target practice.

OVER THE WALL

The colonel was somewhat overenthusiastic, and she wasn't the only one worrying that he had possibly suffered an episode, or maybe she had witnessed the rapid onset of degenerative brain disease.

The man was issuing orders and laughing aloud, but being mostly tolerated by the group, who were busy packing the remaining supplies for their uncertain future outside.

She had long since abandoned her tailored skirt suit and heels and had resorted to the comfortable jumpsuits designed for those living underground for extended periods. Now she was in boots and overalls not unlike a pilot's flight suit, loading a bag and ready to walk out with the others.

It had been years since she had really walked anywhere or carried her own bags, let alone both.

There was a general feel of a plan, but no real plan and certainly no actual leadership. All those senior and important people in one place was bound to cause friction, as most had their ideas which they would then try to bully others into supporting. The world of politics could well end with these few people wasting what remained of their lives arguing, she thought. She would wait until they had established somewhere, then name herself Prime Minister as the most senior cabinet member left.

Everyone carried their own food and water; those who were armed when they came in felt more secure, and she started to notice a shift in the established power balance. For years, these politicians had been protected by armed police officers, and most saw them as part of the furniture-type people; now the politicians stuck to them and started to see them as valuable people. There was no secret weapons cache in the bunker, much to the annoyance of the colonel, who was loudly voicing his hopes that this was a Russian act of war and he would "finally get to stick it to Ivan".

He was pretty much ignored by everyone at the end, including his own kind, some of whom had abandoned the dress uniforms most of them wore in favour of utilitarian clothing.

The time came when they could wait no longer, and, without ceremony, site three opened its sealed steel doors which had protected them for months.

The pressurised door hissed as it was unlocked, letting cool air in from outside. As this happened, one girl from the research team quietly said to herself with a resigned sigh, "We all just died."

THINKING AHEAD

Penny called the group to hush during breakfast, engaging with the regular niceties which Dan wouldn't have bothered with. She looked pale and thinner, he thought. Maybe some time outside would be good for her. Spring was fast approaching, and she explained the needs and expectations of them all.

The priority now was to plant and rear as much as possible during the good weather.

"We will also work on winter-proofing our home for better comfort," she declared. "I'm sure everyone knows we are looking to establish some solar power and possibly hot water when we are equipped to do so. Now, your departmental heads have work for you. Have a good day, everyone."

Chris was by far the busiest; he had limited support. Those assigned to the gardens were equally as busy, but Chris was never really given a break during the busiest time for his trade.

He had given his simplified plan to the council recently: expand their livestock through breeding, get enough feed for them, grow vegetables.

Andrew was in support, and having had a winter to see how the food stores fared, he believed that the farms had three to five years to take over supplying the group before the stocks ran out.

"Dependent on numbers, obviously," he added.

That got Dan thinking: they still needed more of them to make this work. Logistics were stacked with premises to empty, and both crews went on a planned route daily with multiple places to hit.

Engineering had recovered the scaffolding lorries and made a further trip to the distribution place where they had got the lorry full of parts. This time, they returned with thin metal cylinder tanks as well as more panels.

More trees were felled near to the house and dragged to the driveway by tractor to be cut up. The space left was requested by Chris to put pigs in when they were expecting; they could have a steady food supply of kitchen waste then. Steve offered to help and build the fenced pen bit by bit. He said it gave him back a small bit of normality. A semicircular ark was added to the pen for shelter, and the first occupants were herded down the driveway.

Chris wanted his new four-legged assistant to help, but she was still very weak, and Sera said no.

Out of the three puppies, two had died. They were badly malnourished, and frankly the vet marvelled that they had lived as long as they had.

The survivor was a bitch with jet-black fur and a white chin, chest and belly. Ana named her Pig, from a book she had read about a farmer with a sheepdog.

Pig had just about made it through with the milk substitute, and once she could manage solids, she grew much healthier by the day. She was kept inside by Sera until she was happy that the puppy would live; as it was, Pig was going to be a small dog, but there was no way to say for sure if she would be OK in the long term.

Ash was very curious about the little collie sniffing around his paws. He could have fit the entire dog in his mouth easily, yet it scared him and he would jump out of its way. As he became used to this, and Pig grew stronger on her feet, it became an intentional game between them.

Andrew and Liam had started to go out to scavenge again locally, ensuring that every spare storage space was stocked full.

The main aim of the Rangers was to find survivors and recruit, but Steve was set as house guard and trainer for a month. His suggestion was a period of intense firearms training for Leah, then a more relaxed pace from thereon after.

Penny had organised further clearances of the house, opening up another floor of living space as people were asking for their own rooms. The office spaces were emptied and beds brought in; all the unwanted and unusable detritus from the newly reclaimed space went for burning.

In all, the house was a hive of activity with nobody asking for a day off, not that they would have got one.

GREENER GRASS

Kyle lay on the filthy ground where he had been for weeks. His long, wispy beard was matted with something. He didn't know what it was, but a good guess was that it was his own shit. It must be old, because they hadn't fed him for days. He drank when it rained through the holes in the roof to fill his pan up, and every day he wished he had kept his head and not tried to remove Dan's.

He still hated him, even more now that he knew he would die here because of him.

It was his fault, him and his elite followers. A voice inside Kyle told him that not even Dan would treat him like this.

"Shut up!" he shouted back, then slapped a hand over his mouth and froze.

If he shouted, he would be beaten again. *Don't upset them*, he thought to himself; *if you are good and quiet, they might feed you.*

They had fed him well before, when he told them about the group and Dan and his guns. They stopped him then.

"Where are these guns?" the leader, Billy, asked, leaning close to his face. Something in the way he said it made him worry about everyone there and what this man would do to them.

He realised that this man was a bully too; he was like Dan, but this one never pretended to be good.

He tried to politely refuse them, so they beat him. Then they beat him again and again and again.

Then they locked him away, remembering to beat him every so often to wring out any of the minute details he had forgotten to tell them.

He had been in this box for longer than he could remember now, and it was all Dan's fault.

NIKITA

"Begin," said Steve, activating a stopwatch.

Leah drew the Glock and opened the door. She moved in a crouch, which Dan knew was a strain on the legs; she had clearly been working on her strength and fitness.

She moved methodically through the building, which Steve had set up but Leah had never seen before, clearing each room perfectly and quietly. She took the stairs backwards, gun and eyes pointing the same way.

She eventually came to the blind spot where he waited for her. He heard her pause outside the room. He could feel her breathing. A noise to his left made him turn, and as he turned back, he saw Leah had entered the room fast and stood with the gun held level with his chest. She was a little too close, but he was not confident that he could disarm her without getting shot.

He walked outside with her pacing backwards, never losing sight of her target. Joe walked in behind her, shouting, and she turned and pulled the trigger twice. One in the chest, one in the head.

Too late, she turned back to Dan; he was on her, knocking the weapon from her hands. She let her left hand drop away from the gun as she saw this happening and simultaneously drew the knife from her left shoulder strap. Her right hand gripped his vest as the knife was rested against his neck.

"STOP," roared Steve.

She let him go and sheathed the blade before picking up the empty gun and sliding in the magazine from her vest.

She smiled at Dan, then, holstering the gun, she turned to Steve for her assessment.

"How did you know he was there and how did you distract him?" he asked her.

She slipped a hand into a pouch as she said, "It was the last room, and the only place big enough to hide him. Plus, he breathes like an elephant." Then she withdrew her hand from the pouch and produced a small handful of Haribo. "Cost me a cola bottle, though."

Dan laughed, realising the noise was a soft sweet hitting the carpet after she threw it over the door he hid behind. The kid was clever, and fast.

"I'm changing your name to Nikita," he said with a smile.

"Why?" she shot back.

Dan sighed, and Steve promised to find the book.

"Did they make a film of it?" she asked hopefully.

Steve sent her back to the house and filled Dan in as they strolled along.

"Her mile and a half is just over the nine-minute mark," he said, impressed. Dan commented that she was in Paratrooper time.

"She can do pull-ups too. Only a couple at a time, but she's getting fitter. Paul has been working on the hand-to-hand stuff and says that she's getting better by the day," he continued. "She's competent at putting rounds down range, but I'm going to develop that next."

Dan was pleased and thanked Steve for his good work. He was tired, as he'd been taking over on Steve's duty days to give him time to train her.

"I might look for a short-wheelbase Defender for her, and I'll take over for the driving training, if you don't mind?"

Steve didn't. He saw how much Dan cared for the girl and asked him if he had any kids.

Dan was silent for a while as he lit a cigarette. "Girl and a boy. They would have been six and four by now," he said sadly.

"Two boys," Steve shared in return. One was with his mum; the other was away at university.

Dan asked if there was hope there, but Steve told him the last contact he had was to say that he was too ill to come home.

Both full of sadness and regret, they walked on in silence.

MAJOR FEAT OF ENGINEERING

Logistics were reassigned to help the engineering team. The scaffolding went up slowly, and one by one the solar panels were fixed onto a frame of Mike's design. A further trip had to be made for more poles and fixings, and progress was slow.

Mike shared his vision with Dan as he smoked one morning, with Ash playing with Pig and the spaniels around their feet as Pete used a pressurised air rifle to remove a nest of pigeons from the trees marked for felling.

"The A-frame rests over the roof so that we don't have to compromise the integrity of the tiles," Mike explained. "We will hopefully get ten water tanks on the apex to be heated by the top rows, and the rest will power the battery bank. Even better, Adam and Carl are confident that they can fit a power shower in each bathroom."

That was welcome news. Mike went on to explain that he intended to reroute the guttering for a form of toilet flushing and water supply. As he began to explain in more detail, Dan became lost and politely cut him off by saying what a great job he was doing.

"When do you reckon you'll be finished?" Dan asked.

Mike sucked a breath in, performing a practised routine of haggling. Dan was tempted to ask for the straight answer, but found himself playing along.

"Six-month project minimum," Mike started, "and that's not taking into account any bad weather or technical problems…"

"Cut the bullshit; what's this going to cost me?" Dan said in jest, making Mike laugh. "Just let me know if you need anything," Dan finished before he walked away, calling Ash to stop playing and follow.

He was happy with the engineering side, but was worried about Chris. He looked very tired and had been working long hours with Ana on the farm. Pete had taken days at a time off hunting to help him.

He decided that the Rangers' new priority was another recruitment drive. He walked into Ops to see Lexi and Joe kitting up for their tasks.

"New objective, people," he declared confidently as he strode in, "find more survivors. We need more hands here, and we've been focusing too internally."

They looked at each other, then back to Dan to accept their new task.

"Take an extra jerrycan of diesel and try to stay out as long as you can; be careful," he said, then opened a map to give them directions so as not to overlap.

He kitted up himself and called Ash to him. He put Ash's Christmas E&E dog vest on him with a spare water bottle and packet of food and went to tell Steve where they were going.

HAPPINESS IS PURPOSE

He didn't really know how to explain it, not without upsetting people, but Joe was happier now than he had ever been. Not at first, not when he was sleeping on the floor of his shop and waiting for someone to tell him what to do, but now. Right now, this very moment, was the best moment of his life so far.

He had been a failure before. He'd tried hard but just wasn't good enough. So they said.

Now he was driving a hard-core truck, and carrying an assault rifle and a handgun. Not only did he have all this great stuff, but he now knew how to use it.

Joe was under no illusion that he was great; Dan and Steve were both ex-military – that was obvious. Lexi was fit and could fight, plus she'd already proven herself. He never mentioned this, in case the thought of stencilling a bad guy on the wing of your Land Rover was distasteful. Shit, even the vet had seen more action than him.

He wasn't immature about it, and certainly wasn't out to look for trouble, but he wanted to prove himself. He was fitter, stronger and more capable to handle himself than ever before. He practised with his weapons until he was confident in himself. The only remaining test was a real-life scenario.

If he followed the instructions from Dan and Steve, he would avoid problems. That wouldn't prove his worth much, but he was determined not to screw up.

He drove west, and after an hour started stopping at the places most likely to have attracted survivors. He found evidence of people having looted, indicating survivors had been there, but no evidence of people still there.

Another hour and still no sign of life. By lunchtime, he had crossed into Wales and struck gold.

In truth, they found him, not the other way around.

He drove along a lane into a village and was so surprised to see another vehicle coming towards him that he didn't react straight away.

The other car, a normal family estate, stopped in the road. Joe stopped and the two had a standoff for a few seconds.

Joe forced himself to think: what was he supposed to do now? He had expected to find grateful people huddled in terrible conditions waiting for rescue.

The driver of the estate acted first, by reversing away. Joe snapped out of his daze and dropped his own vehicle into gear to follow. He flashed his lights desperately, trying to get them to stop. They didn't, and after a poorly executed J-turn, they were pursued by Joe to a campsite. The occupants of the car – two young women he saw – fled behind the buildings shouting.

A booming sound echoed out as a woman appeared from the side of a caravan, lowering a shotgun to point it at Joe.

He was sure this was a defensive thing and that they were not attacking him. He switched off his engine and slowly climbed out of his cab, keeping both hands up. He had the Glock on his right leg and had intentionally left the rifle out of sight.

The woman with the shotgun came towards him, scared and desperate. He started to talk but she screamed at him to shut up. "You tell him we are not his property!" she said, confusing Joe.

"Who?" he asked.

"You know full well who I'm talking about. That bastard wants girls; no amount of threats will make us get on our backs for him. Now fuck off and tell him that," she said, snarling at him.

"Look," he said reasonably, "I'm nothing to do with anyone here. I've come from miles away looking for more survivors."

She glared at him, considering the possibility that she had been wrong.

"Seriously," Joe said, "I've never been here before and you are the first people I have spoken to since I left home today."

She thought about this and asked, "How many of you? Where?"

"Feel free to put that down and I'll tell you everything," he countered reasonably.

"No," she snapped. "You're still armed."

"Fine," said Joe, turning his right leg towards her. "Take it, but I'm not your enemy."

She studied him for a bit longer, then abruptly lowered the shotgun.

"Talk, then," she said impatiently.

Joe told her his story from the start, quickly catching up to today. As he spoke, the two women from the car appeared and listened intently.

The woman gave a gruff account of how they had found each other in the days since, and had lived off the village in this campsite until winter forced them to look further away. That led them into a neighbouring town where they first met "King" Pat. He had a dozen followers – shabby little boys really – but they did whatever he told them to do.

"We call him Fagin. You know, like in *Oliver Twist*?" she said. Joe knew. "He told us we had trespassed in his kingdom and that we had to serve him or pay the price."

The price turned out to be that they "work" for him. She refused, and they had been hunted for nearly two weeks.

"We can help," Joe said. "Come with me."

FAGIN

Joe made two mistakes.

First, he didn't notice the vehicle that had followed him.

Second, he didn't tune in to the sound of another three vehicles approaching as they talked.

By the time he noticed, it was too late. They were in the campsite.

The woman screamed that Joe had led them to her. He ignored her and took action to make up for his failure in observations.

He drew the Glock and emptied the magazine into the radiator of the lead vehicle, sure that he was right to resist this self-proclaimed King.

The car stopped, blocking the gateway, as water poured from the underside of the engine. That wouldn't be moving anywhere soon. The woman fired her remaining loaded cartridge into the windscreen, peppering it with spider webs as the shatterproof glass held.

Joe yelled at her for another way out.

"Field," she yelled, pointing behind the buildings. "Yours will make it, but ours won't."

"Get the girls in. Now," he said to her as he retrieved his rifle from the cab.

As he rounded the Defender and levelled the gun, a voice rang out from behind the crippled roadblock.

"You in there with the gun," it bawled, full of scorn and cruelty. "Those women are my property. Everything here is my property, and you are trespassing on my sovereignty."

He turned to see the three women dragging another with handfuls of possessions. The one with the gun bundled the others inside and turned to Joe.

"That's the bastard," she said angrily.

"Tell me about the way out," he said.

"Field. Leads back to the road. About a mile but rough ground."

Joe's thoughts were pulled back to the blocked entrance, where King Fagin began shouting orders which would leave them flanked.

He fired ten carefully placed rounds at the other cars. Some ricocheted off wheel rims, but most connected. He put two into the only other exposed grill, which was the one furthest away. Satisfied that they would not be chased – not by these cars anyway – he jumped in and started the Land Rover. The women were all shouting at once, and he was fairly certain that none of them trusted him.

He drove carefully over the uneven ground but still bounced his passengers around to their annoyance. He turned to the woman in the passenger seat and asked if her shotgun was reloaded.

"No. I've just used the last two cartridges we had."

He paused when they reached the road and reloaded both of his weapons. He pushed the gate open with the vehicle, breaking the fixings easily, and sped down the road to put distance between them and the last place they were seen.

He shouted over the noise of the unhappy passengers and asked for directions towards England.

~

King Patrick was fuming. How dare a trespasser step foot on his land and take his possessions? How dare he fire a gun at his boys? He looked at the wreckage of three cars that would never drive again, angry.

He vowed to find this thief and hang him for his crimes. He sent his cleverest boys to follow them on a motorbike. He would find him.

~

Joe drove hard for twenty minutes, before stopping and pulling the Defender off the road. He took his rifle and told the women to wait there. He had to be sure he wasn't followed.

He set himself up with a good view of the road, and after a few minutes, he heard an engine. As it came into sight, he saw a teenage boy coming slowly, clearly looking to follow them. He couldn't let that happen.

He hoped he was right, and pulled the trigger.

UNHAPPY CAMPERS

Lexi drove for hours, checking supermarkets and fuel stations as she wove her way southwest. She eventually saw signs of life in looted shops. Worryingly, she saw markings painted on buildings, thinking nothing of them at first, but the more she saw, the more they looked like territorial symbols.

She went slowly, senses on alert, until she saw the same markings painted on a vehicle which wasn't covered with the winter grime of the others.

She pulled up nearby and sounded the horn twice. She figured if she didn't like the look of anyone who came out, then she could drive away.

Two men appeared carrying boxes. They saw Lexi's Land Rover and stared, then seemed to be arguing between themselves for a while before the younger-looking one of the two was sent over. He approached cautiously, and Lexi drew her sidearm slowly and rested it in her lap. She kept the doors locked and wound down the passenger window halfway.

He looked nervous and asked her who sent her.

"Nobody sent me here. I'm out looking for people to join us," she replied.

"We're not finished here and we have to get our quota or we don't eat. You're not one of Bronson's, so who are you?" he said.

"I don't know who Bronson is, and I'm not from around here," Lexi said. "What do you mean by 'quota'?"

He seemed annoyed but glanced at her equipment as he spoke. "We have to find a certain amount each day to get fed – that's how it works if you want to avoid punishment."

Lexi lit a smoke and looked straight at him. "We don't have quotas, and all of us eat three times a day. Reckon you and your mate want some of that?"

He thought for a second, then ran over to the bigger man and had another argument which went on longer.

The smaller one came back to her.

"I'm in, but Ed is worried about the others," he explained. Lexi raised an eyebrow to ask more.

"Bronson has loads of people, but he uses enforcers to keep us in line. If we run off, what happens to them?" he said.

"I don't know," she said. "If people are being kept prisoner by him, then we can help. We'd need you to come back and tell us everything you know, though."

"There aren't enough of you to take him on, I bet. He's got gangs of thugs and some of them have guns too," the man said in a whine.

Lexi smiled and patted her M4, which lay on the dash. "Trust me, my lot is not to be messed with, either."

He thought a while longer, then ran over to his friend. They spoke again, and this time they both walked over to her.

"You reckon you can help?" asked the bigger man cynically. "He's got twenty or more people my size; he even tried to make me one of them, but I don't like hurting people for fun."

"Yes," she said confidently. "We've seen our fair share of bad ones, and it didn't go well for them."

They looked between themselves and silently agreed to escape. Ed looked back to Lexi. "I'm Ed, and this is James."

"Get in, boys," she said, starting the Land Rover.

SMALL VICTORIES

Dan drove north, skirting the edges of the city that Marie had described as being full of pirates. He saw a car garage with things in the window he used to dream of; the overwhelming urge to steal a McLaren almost overcame him, until he shook himself out of the daydream.

"One day, boy," he said to Ash, receiving a puzzled look from the dog.

He parked on an overpass and got out. Ash watered the tyres while Dan sat and smoked. From his vantage point, he could see for miles, and one direction led to an unbroken series of buildings which led all the way to the city centre. He had no intention of heading that way, not without more trigger fingers on his side.

He listened for sounds of anything human, but as the sun sank lower in the distance, he felt very alone.

He gave up on the perch and drove through the housing estates. Lines of newly built Lego houses sat on a former factory site, something which the developer was trying to turn into romanticism. He thought they were still lifeless new builds on the outskirts of a shithole of an area.

Not a single sign of anyone living was seen: no looted shops or cleared roads, nothing.

He stopped again and consulted the map, planning a longer route home which led him through farmland for miles.

As he drove, his mind wandered slightly, his thoughts as they often did turning to Marie. A small wave of guilt brought him back to the present in time for his eyes to register a pillar of smoke in the distance.

He pointed it out to Ash, who didn't care at all, and made his way towards it. The source of the fire was a small pile of burning bodies, shrunk to the size of children as the heat got to the bones.

He had approached as quietly as he could, but there was nobody in sight. He was destined to have a lonely day, it seemed.

An engine note pierced the sound of the fire as a tractor turned off the road towards them. He decided on the gentle approach and slung the carbine behind him. The tractor slowed as the driver saw him but still came on cautiously. He made Ash sit, and he strolled to meet the driver.

He was taken aback slightly when the man driving it jumped down. Literally.

Dan placed him at five feet tall at best. In heels. He had a red face, was jug-eared, and the word *pugnacious* sprang instantly to mind. To make him sound as comical as he looked, he had a high-pitched Welsh accent.

The formalities were conducted, and Ewan asked questions about the group.

"You got enough people looking after the farm?" he asked as nonchalantly as he could.

"No, as it happens," said Dan.

They spoke some more; Ewan knew where the prison was, and he agreed to make his way there tomorrow with all of his supplies. Dan suspected him to be a resentful man and a bit of a loner, probably having spent his life in jealous anger at people like himself – taller people.

He said that he had barely survived winter, and was struggling to plant crops alone. He warmed slightly, and was genuinely happy at the thought of a bigger farm and company.

Dan left him to it and they shook hands with a promise to meet tomorrow. He was conscious not to bend down to him to do it. Dan made his way home leisurely over the next hour, only to pull up in his "spot" near the front door to see Joe's Defender abandoned there, still with a door open. Dan glanced inside the cab, looking for blood and being slightly relieved to see none.

Worried that something was wrong, he burst inside to see a gaggle of people in Ops around a flustered Joe. He looked relieved to see Dan, who wanted to know what was happening. Conscious that Joe had never had a "contact", he gestured with his head for him to join him in his room.

Dan went carefully with Joe, poured two single malts, and let him go at his own pace. Joe drank, calmed his nerves, and his breathing began to even out. He thought Joe might just be as scared of him as he was of the outside world, and he didn't want that.

"From the beginning, Joe," he said softly.

"Crossed over into Wales mid-afternoon, saw a car. It took off, so I followed. Found the four women in an abandoned caravan park. Turns out the area was 'claimed' by some twat who calls himself the 'King.' The women call him Fagin because he gets boys to do his dirty

116

work." Joe took another sip. "They got the drop on me," he said, using one of Dan's terms, "and I had to react."

Dan paused, letting the report sink in. Joe had found multiple female survivors, then been ambushed by a nutcase and his gang of children. He was impressed that Joe made it back, let alone bringing four women out.

"Go on," Dan said.

"They came in a tight bunch of three cars. I emptied the Glock into the radiator of the first one, then got my rifle and took out the tyres of the others and the radiator of the back one so all the cars were stuck," he finished, almost breathless.

Dan was impressed. "Quick thinking. I'm going to have to add that move to the handbook," he said without a trace of sarcasm.

Joe looked up, relieved because he thought he had screwed up. In truth, he had, but Dan was in no mood to point that out, as Joe was suffering enough with his first big post-adrenaline report as it was.

"We went cross-country to get away. I put in a dogleg" – Dan's term for ambushing your own trail – "and one followed on a motorbike, looking to hang back. I couldn't risk him finding this place, so I…" He stopped.

"So you put him down?" Dan asked.

Joe just nodded as the tears came. Dan felt for him. He knew that familiar outpouring of stress after a fight or a contact, knew how grown men, no matter how tough, were susceptible to the emotional drain of it.

"You did bloody well at the campsite. It showed quick thinking and tactical planning. I'm impressed," Dan said. "And you were absolutely right to protect this place from some dickhead who thinks he's royalty; you were right to put him down," he finished firmly, trying to reassure Joe.

Joe wasn't doing much talking back right now, so Dan changed the subject slightly. "How many rounds?" he asked firmly.

"Entire mag from the Glock: fifteen nine mils. Eleven from the rifle, all on single fire. No misses."

Talking bullets seemed to have woken him up a little. Dan stood.

"Good work. Clean your guns and report to Marie."

Joe started to object, saying that he was fine.

Dan cut him off. "It's mandatory following a contact; I know you're OK, but we have to stick to the rules."

"OK, boss," said Joe as he stood to leave.

Dan dashed upstairs to find Marie before Joe could put her on the spot about the "mandatory" counselling after a contact, as he had just made it up.

He found her, muttered in her ear that Joe had fired his weapons today and killed a hostile. She took the news calmly, asking if he had done the right thing.

"He absolutely did, but he fucked up by letting them get that close in the first place. He has to know he reacted well and saved lives, OK?" Dan pulled away from her, thinking that she still smelled good even after the world ended.

She smiled at him and nodded. He didn't know what else to say to her so he went, leaving her watching him. He always felt very shabby in her company.

He went back downstairs to let Ash out, just as Lexi returned.

SURVEILLANCE

The second boy on his scrambler bike found his friend in the road. He thought he had crashed to start with, but as he turned him over and called his name, he saw a black stain on his clothing where the bullet had punched through his chest. His lip trembled, and he fought back the urge to cry. His fear and sadness turned slowly to anger, anger at the murder of his brother and the invader who had come and shamed them all.

He took what he wanted from the pockets and bag of his now deceased brother, taking over the heavy burden of his mission.

He would follow the bastard back to his home. He would not be caught out like his friend, who was chosen above him. He would bring the news back to the King and he would be rewarded.

He followed carefully, stopping to scout ahead and waiting for movement in the distance. Twice more he saw the big off-roader stop, and twice he held his position in silence until the bastard had given up waiting and driven on again. He felt more confident to stay closer after there was no third stop, no longer fearing a bullet as he rode along. He cut his engine as he rolled down the hills after them, crossing over into the next country with no regard for territory or boundaries.

For hours, he shadowed their moves, always staying far enough behind to not be seen. He followed the sound and the smell of the vehicle at times when the views were obstructed, only to have to catch up when the geography allowed. It was hard work, but he stayed with them until he lost the Land Rover on a stretch of road. He went ahead before doubling back, sure that they had to have turned off somewhere within a one-mile stretch.

He stopped his bike and listened. He heard animals, machinery, and a small burst of laughter drifted to him on a breeze, gone as soon as it was recognised.

This had to be the place, he thought. He waited, hiding himself and his bike in some trees. He did not have to wait long until he was rewarded with the sound of another vehicle. A big black Discovery rolled along the road past him. It was a piece of artwork, with bigger wheels and custom roof rack and bumpers; someone had spent a lot of money on that. He laughed to himself. Like any of that mattered any more. He watched as the big truck turned into a junction towards the noises he heard. *A prison: that's where they've set up shop.* He waited longer, to be thorough. Another Land Rover came in shortly afterwards with a girl driving and two others in the vehicle. This place was well equipped, he reckoned.

He started his bike and retraced his steps, having to stop to fill up his tank using the hosepipe he carried just before crossing into his home country. He rode fast, trying to use the last of the daylight to get back, finding the wreckage of his friend's dropped bike still where he left it. His body was gone.

The noise of his bike made people look up at his arrival. He ignored the questions about where he had been and what he knew. He took his news straight to the King.

"Your Highness," he called loudly, dropping to one knee as the two most trusted of them eyed him with scorn. They puffed themselves up, forcing their dominance on him. They knew their friend was dead, and this one now returned with news. The King rewarded good news, and they had none to offer where he obviously did. He would be climbing the food chain tonight, and they didn't like it.

"Come up, boy," said his Highness, King Patrick, from his seat on the raised platform.

He did. He told his King everything he had learned.

MORE ENEMIES THAN FRIENDS

Lexi brought two men back with her who carried nothing with them. Concerned, Dan asked if she had run into any trouble as she introduced them.

"No, but you'll want to hear what these two have to say," she said, explaining briefly.

James was young and slim, whereas the other man was big, like Kev's size. They were taken away for induction with the women and Dan told Lexi what had happened to Joe. She was shocked, and asked him if Joe was OK.

"He will be. I've sent him to see Marie, which is standard practice following a contact now. As of twenty minutes ago, anyway," he added subtly.

Lexi didn't argue with that, having spent valuable time talking through her first killing to better come to terms with it.

He told her of the farmer he had found, who should be joining them tomorrow.

"I still want a guard posted for when he gets here, though," he said, voicing his constant worries that they were an attractive target for others.

He stowed his gear in his room, putting a bowl of food down for Ash, then went into the house.

With James and Ed were four stressed-looking women. He was given their names, but it was done so quickly that he had no time to set them in his mind before they were breezed away for a tour.

They went into Ops to speak to Steve and Leah; Dan wanted a plan before one was requested of him. He filled them in, and as he spoke, Leah got out a large-scale map of the area which had their location marked and numerous little coloured dots.

Joe's trip into Wales had a simple enough answer: avoid the place.

Dan assumed that the "kingdom" Joe spoke of would no doubt expand in the future, so he drew on a map of the area making the limit of their journeys west about twenty miles short of the border. There was no pressing need to encroach on another large group's territory in this case. Let this lunatic take over the country for now; it would be years before it came to wars of the cattle raids that told the backstory of the neighbouring countries.

Lexi's trip concerned Dan far more; if people grouped together and pooled supplies for a common good, then he thought that was great. They could even trade with them in the future. If, however, people in that group were being threatened and exploited by others using force, then Dan swore to himself that it would be stopped. Slavery still had no place in the world in his opinion, even if the laws on murder and torture were slightly more relaxed nowadays.

He needed to get the two from there in to be thoroughly de-briefed, but gently so as not to make them feel that they swapped one dictatorship for another.

Lexi showed them the place on the map where she picked them up, an industrial area on an estuary near to a large docks and a sprawling city.

"Leah," he said, surprising the girl, whose thoughts had wandered off. "Fire up that laptop and bring up the maps. I want a better look at this place."

She was excited, as she had not yet had a reason to use something that had been scavenged from a library. It was a CD version of a world atlas, archived from a time before technology gave everyone a detailed map of the world courtesy of smartphones and the Internet. A couple of years out of date, maybe, but in the absence of Google Earth, it gave a much better picture with roads overlaid on the satellite imagery.

"Kings and militant dictatorships," Dan muttered to nobody in particular. "This country just turned into tribal Africa overnight."

HUMAN RESOURCES

Penny had done her normal evening routine of welcoming the new survivors to the group, only this newest lot seemed more traumatised than previous arrivals. Maybe it was spending the winter alone and barely surviving that made them seem less excited, or the other survivors they had met who weren't so kind to them.

Penny called the council heads to stay and invited Karen to give another rundown of the skills and capabilities as she had before. This time, there was no sense of hierarchy with the woman: she was just happy doing her job.

The four women brought back by Joe were discussed first. Laura, a bank clerk in her early thirties, had seemingly held the group together and led them through winter by keeping them ahead of more unfriendly survivors. She was tough, a leader, but had no skill set to bring, really. Thoughts were invited from the group as to who wanted her.

Jimmy cleared his throat. "Is she the type for a bit of manual labour? I'm still one down since Kyle, um, left. If she's switched on and capable, I'll take her to head up another logistics crew?" It was agreed to make the offer to her.

Karen moved on. "Melissa. Eighteen, should have finished A levels last year. Grew up in the country. She has expressed interest in the animals."

"Sold," said Chris straight away. They all knew he had more work than helping hands, and the spring would only pile more on him.

Karen nodded. "In that case, maybe you'll like that her close friend is almost inseparable from her." She checked her notes again. "Kerry is twenty-two and was a biology student in her final year after a 'break' where she travelled to South America. She has knowledge of genetics and wants to stay with Melissa if you would like her too?" She looked at Chris.

"Definitely. She can work out breeding programmes and track our herd growth."

"Lovely," said Karen, who found animals quite disgusting.

Dan saw the look on her face and reminded himself to scare her with his "monstrosity" of a dog that she liked so much when he next got the opportunity.

"Nina ran a small catering franchise and has a desire to stay in that line of work."

"I could do with some help," said Cara quickly, still slightly nervous at having a senior role to play.

"Moving on, neither James nor Ed have asked for placements. James worked in a call centre, but did grow up shooting and fishing."

Dan looked to Chris, as he was the one who spoke to Pete most. "Apprentice gamekeeper?" he suggested. Chris was happy with the idea, as were the others.

"I'll take the big guy," Dan said.

Karen opened her mouth to speak, but Penny interjected. "It seems we have recruited our first true pacifist," she said with a soft smile. "The only thing he wants no part of is violence, and it seems that his captors had wanted to recruit him into their enforcement ranks. He was beaten for refusing, even though it would have meant more food and better conditions. He refuses to hurt people on principle."

Dan was shocked. It was the kind of justification he had heard from six-stone women who didn't eat cheese, as the milk was stolen from cows. He knew it wasn't the same thing, and he felt a little understanding for the man.

"OK then!" he said, lost for more words.

Pig yapped at Chris, conveying boredom at being stuck inside, but it stirred him enough to ask if Ed would join the gardens. "We've got a need for a heavy lifter, and work will pick up there soon, as things need planting."

Dan told them of the farmer he had met and warned them all about his unique appearance.

Chris stirred again. "Welshman?" he asked.

"Yeah. You know him?" Dan said.

"I think so, from Young Farmers years ago. Hard to think there'd be two who look like him!" Chris was happy for another experienced man on the farm, and said he would see how he got on with a view to making Ewan a foreman.

Penny nodded to Karen, who took it as a polite dismissal. She would go and speak to the new ones about their work.

Penny started in again after Karen had left.

"There are concerns about where these people came from. Clearly the women were hiding from a self-styled King of Wales, but I'm assured they will not be able to follow them here." She looked at Dan, who nodded.

"Joe took care of that," he said. "He's a bit tender about it and needs to let it sink in, but he did well. The others are more of a worry."

Everyone listened in more carefully.

"I want to question James and his mate in detail, as it seems they were basically slaves in a large group where they employ enforcers to make them scavenge for them. God knows what is going on there, but I don't like it. Not one bit." Frowns and head shakes rippled around the table. Dan went on. "Based on what they say, I may feel the need to visit their 'leader' and explain why slavery was abolished."

The threat hung heavy in the air as they all went away to their own thoughts.

BUNKER BUSTER

They had stepped out into the world for the first time in months to find a wasteland. Rubbish swirled around the streets; cars lay on flat wheels covered in winter grime. Their plan to get a vehicle failed, as none were well enough preserved, resulting in a convoy of traipsing people heading for a nearby army barracks. Some of the group simply walked off alone, desperate hopes of finding loved ones running through their heads.

Most of the group eventually reached the barracks, where the now-delirious colonel yelled at the long-dead Ministry of Defence police barrier guard to open the gates. Some of them broke in and found the place partly ransacked. With no way of opening the weapons lockers without power, they took what they found lying around. They set themselves up in the mess area, where people found what food was still edible.

There was no cohesion, no leadership, and no purpose.

She felt forlorn, uncomfortable in her clothes, and scared. She tried to call them to order to hear her carefully planned speech, which had actually been written by her as they walked and not by one of her staff as she had been used to for years now.

Without a speaker to call the assembled people to order, she was ignored. One of the remaining police officers even shouted at her and called her an "interfering bitch". She knew to expect such vulgarity from them; she would have wiped them all away to replace them with private companies working to government policy if she still had the power.

Only now she had nothing, and the realisation crushed her.

She lay on the comfortable seats and rested. She coughed, the force of it getting away from her, and ended up doubling her over in a coughing fit. When she finally caught her breath and wiped the tears from her eyes, she saw them all looking at her in horrified silence. Those near her didn't even have the tact to slide away slowly: they just got up and moved quickly, giving her a stare.

She felt like a leper, and her head spun as her body temperature started to rise. One by one, the rest of the group started to cough.

ENTER THE DRAGON

Ewan arrived just after breakfast, driving a big continental tractor – the kind that could do normal road speeds – and towing a large trailer. Chris met him, and the two recognised each other immediately. Ewan was offered the tour but refused, saying that he had set off before dawn and needed help bringing back machinery that they would need. All available people were tasked to go back and bring what they could. Steve drove their old minibus with a view to dumping it there and driving something more useful back.

Ewan saw the scaffolding at the front of the house and asked if they were conned by some fascia salesman.

The solar panel work was explained to him, and Chris admitted that it was slow progress, as the panels had to be carefully lifted one at a time.

"Bollocks, man!" said Ewan. "Get that Manitou" – the big telescopic forklift on the farm was apparently called a Manitou – "up here and lift the whole pallet!"

How that had escaped the entire engineering team was a mystery to Dan, but it seemed like the strange-looking and slightly obnoxious Welshman was going to be helpful.

He smiled at the small man giving a loud explanation of what he would do if he were building it and walked inside.

Leah was in Ops, having got hold of a nervous-looking James and Ed as she was asked to. Dan sat down with them and gathered a notepad and pen close as Leah worked the map on the laptop.

"Thanks for coming in, gents," he started in a friendly tone. "I know this sounds silly, but you aren't in any trouble." Both relaxed slightly. "You've got jobs now, I hear?" he asked, to warm them up a little.

James spoke first. "I've got to work with Pete and learn more about gamekeeping," he said. He was happy about that.

"I'm going to be a gardener and grow vegetables," said Ed as happily as he could, still quite suspicious of Dan.

"Good stuff. If it doesn't work out, or you want to learn something new instead, just ask Chris," he said, ending the ice breaking. "Now, I need to know more about where you came from and I'll be completely up front about it: if people are keeping slaves to work for them, then I intend to put a stop to it if I can."

Ed studied the man in front of him. For all his smiles, he still looked dangerous. Ed was taller and probably had four stone on him in weight, but he was scared of him. He had a vicious scar down the left side of his face which Ed doubted was a shaving accident.

Without doubt, this Dan was a fighter. As much as fighting upset and offended him, he wanted the others to be free too.

James began telling Dan all about who was in charge and how many thugs he had with him. He told him about the shipping containers they lived in, and that they couldn't get out unless the crane lifted them. They were fed and let out to work. In the winter, they had metal barrels for fires and kept warm, but they were still prisoners. He would not think about what punishment the others had received after they didn't come back.

Dan asked questions about the layout, the guards and their shifts, what weapons they carried. He wanted the guns described in detail, and asked insignificant questions about how the leader and the guards talked to each other, whether they used any jargon or code words, and if they had radios. This went on for over an hour as Dan wrote pages of notes. The kid, who was dressed like one of the soldiers, was working on a laptop and found the shipping yard. He studied the pictures as she gave James a big piece of blank paper and asked him to draw the place where the shipping containers were. She asked questions as Dan looked over the map, checking against a paper one as he went.

The girl got James to mark where the guards stayed, where they walked, and lots of other drips of information.

Their questioning finally came to an end, but before they left, Dan said, "One last thing, boys. If I go and set your friends free, I'll need you to come and convince them they are going to be safe."

For maybe the fourth time during the questions, Ed spoke. "I'll come to see those people safe, but I'll not take part in anything that comes before. OK?"

"Understood, Ed. Loud and clear," Dan replied.

Dan and Leah were left alone. He went over his notes and let out a sigh. Leah looked at him and he summarised.

"Thirty-plus survivors kept as slaves. Up to twenty guards with a range of weapons including at least five shotguns, a rifle and two semiautomatic pistols. High ground approach, but to a dead end."

He stopped and rubbed his face, scratching the stiff scar down his left eye.

"This isn't going to be easy, kid," he said.

"You'll figure it out; you always do," she said helpfully. "I'll make a model of their camp," she declared as she skipped off to find Marie, who was teaching her how to draw in their sessions.

"Oh, if I had your faith in me," he said to himself as Boris jumped onto his notes and hissed at him.

HOT SHOWERS

With help from Ewan over the next week, the pitched roof was now mostly covered on both sides by solar panels. Eight metal tanks lined the apex, all firmly connected to the scaffolding frame which was being secured wherever they could. Pipes ran down to the two bathrooms and the kitchen where Adam had fitted new taps. Heavy wires wrapped in rolls of tape snaked back up, powering the battery bank, which in turn fed electricity to the house.

Mike said it wasn't an endless supply, and suggested a further scaffold tower or two be erected on the flat ground near the house. More materials were required for this, as well as a smaller but similar setup for the farm and gardens, and teams were deployed to recover what he needed.

The big win was what Adam and Carl had done: the rainwater reservoir tanks fitted to the guttering system now filled the uppermost floor of the house, and the newly fitted electric showers – three in each bathroom – were ready for use.

Marie was the most excited, claiming she hadn't washed her hair properly for nearly a year, and organised an official opening ceremony. A ribbon was found and cut in lighthearted mockery of their old lives, and the queues went along the corridor. Neil had to use the generators to boost the power supply, as the solar panels hadn't yet had a chance to fully charge the batteries.

Dan was amazed at how the small things in life, like a hot shower, made everyone happy. Happy was good. Happy was productive.

The new hands had made the farming and gardening tasks much easier. They had four polytunnels of potatoes growing and a handful of other vegetables which could be grown early. Ewan had been a godsend in that respect, as he brought sacks of mouldy potatoes sprouting lank shoots and they had gone in the ground to make a new crop. His return trips had also yielded pigs, a cockerel and some chickens, and more cows as well as some pieces of farm machinery which made work quicker.

The general feeling was good, and people went about their daily routines with a smile.

Dan brooded, saving his own thoughts of the impending conflict for only a few who knew what he was planning.

His Rangers went out, scouting the things he needed. He tried different scenarios out in his head, calculating problems and losses. That was the issue: he couldn't serve up a plan to the council which allowed for any losses.

He theorised with Steve over Leah's cardboard model; they pored over the maps and suggested different plans of attack which the others were invited to criticise.

Leah surprised him by saying, "Why don't you just go and ask them to let the people go?"

The stunned silence was broken by Steve laughing.

Leah looked annoyed and snapped at him. "That's just the start, but if you're going to laugh, then I won't tell you!"

Dan looked at her more closely. She had an idea, and she had the balls to offer it in their company.

"Run me through it, kid," he said.

WAR GAMES

"Drive straight up to the gate and ask to talk to their boss," she explained. "You'll have top cover here and here," she said impatiently, pointing at two marks on her model. "All of the people we want to rescue will be inside metal containers, so they won't get shot by accident," she said, as though she spoke to a child in a weird role reversal. "If they say no, then you shoot the guards on the top – never more than eight to ten – and deal with the rest coming from where their building is." She was annoyed because it was the fifth time she had talked him through it step by step.

He thought about it. "How do we know they'll all be there?" he asked.

She flipped the laptop around, showing her now typed notes of the debrief. "No night activity, and all guards sleep in an adjacent building bar the ones watching the pen. We get there for sunrise and they'll be there," she finished with a triumphant look.

Dan looked to the other Rangers sitting around the table. "Leah," he said carefully, "do you realise your plan involves killing twenty or so people?"

"Yes. But they aren't nice people, and they aren't coming to live here."

He couldn't argue with her logic, but he worried that he may have created a monster. "How am I supposed to 'deal' with more than ten people rushing out shooting at me, even assuming that the ones on guard duty have been shot?" he asked, fearing the answer.

"Machine gun. In the back of a truck like in the films," she said with finality.

He hated to admit it, but she had come up with a simple plan which had every possibility of working. Their plans all fell down when they tried to extract scared people without confronting their captors.

"There's a lot more to it, but fundamentally I think she's right," said Steve carefully. Leah practically burst with smug pride.

"OK, everyone think on it, but keep it to yourselves," Dan said as they left. He called Steve back and asked him if he thought Leah was too quick to suggest killing. "I haven't pushed her too far, have I?" he asked.

Steve had spent a lot of time with her as her training progressed and knew her well. "No. She's looking at this as a problem to be solved using what we have. She was never constrained by rules of engagement before, and never will be now. She's not a psychopath; she's being pragmatic like you. Albeit a little cold…"

Dan laughed. "Mount the GPMG in the back of a truck like in the films! What's she been watching?"

Steve laughed with him and poured two glasses from the bottle he retrieved from a drawer. "It has its merits and is entirely doable. Personally, I'd like more evidence that they are actually mistreating people. I'd like eyes on myself, ideally."

"Me too, but the risk is too high," said Dan as he sipped. "I'll work it out, and see if Neil can weld a tripod into a Defender! In the meantime, train her hard tomorrow; she's getting cocky."

His head swam with possible tweaks to her plan, but essentially she was right: get everyone in place, demand they release the people, and kill them if they didn't. They still had to then calm and rescue the people inside and take responsibility for them – after all, they had been dependent on the bastards for food and shelter and probably wouldn't know how to look after themselves. He was planning to kill twenty and bring back over thirty.

What if they didn't want to be here? What if they wanted to stay where they were? What if some of them knew the guards or were related to them?

After breakfast, Dan walked outside with Ash; it was just about warm enough for shirtsleeves, but his body armour gave him another layer. He smoked as he walked up to the farm to find Neil in his workshop.

"Wotcha, old bean," Neil said cheerfully from under the bonnet of a Defender he was servicing.

Ash ran to him and sniffed his pockets until he gave up his work, giggling, and tossed him a treat. Neil always had some on him, as the group now had four dogs. All of them liked him, which was no surprise at all based on the contents of his pockets.

"Hypothetical question, mate," Dan said, getting a well-deserved sceptical look. "Is it possible to mount the GPMG on a Land Rover?"

"Of course it's possible, but this ain't Desert bloody Storm! What the hell are you planning, mate?"

Dan's mind flashed to pictures of the "pinkies" with GPMGs on each side and a fifty calibre in the back. He didn't keep secrets from Neil and trusted him not to gossip.

"I want to rescue those people to the south, and we don't have the numbers to take them on conventionally. We need to surprise them with overwhelming force," he said. He ran through the basics of Leah's plan, and told him what he imagined for the heavy gun.

Neil mulled it over. "It's a bit cold-blooded, isn't it?" he asked.

Dan told him it was a teenage girl who suggested it.

"You've cloned yourself!" Neil laughed, then faded off to his thoughts.

"If you're serious, I can do it. I need a long-wheelbase pickup with a removable tin back, like the farm ones."

"Done," said Dan, and he left Neil to his tinkering.

"Bring that flash Disco of yours in for an oil change too," Neil shouted after him.

Dan walked through the farm, keeping Ash close. He saw Chris and Ewan deep in conversation by a large lean-to – basically a three-sided barn where the spare vehicles had been stored. Pig saw them first and bounced over to play with Ash and lick at his face until he swatted a huge paw at her and played. She was small for a collie, not much bigger than Pete's cockers, but considering her early life, she was lucky to be alive. She always stayed close to Chris with an unquestioning loyalty.

Dan spoke with them for a while, hearing their plans for the farm over the coming years.

Chris seemed awkward after Ewan left them, and asked Dan, "What's this I'm hearing about a rescue mission?"

He wasn't entirely shocked that people had talked, but was certain it hadn't come from his Rangers, so people wouldn't know how they planned to do it.

"I'm going to suggest it, yes. Our cattle are kept better than they are, from what we've heard."

Chris was pleased and offered any help he could provide.

"I might need everyone who knows how to use a shotgun to stand guard if we all go. I think I'll need all the Rangers on this one," Dan said.

"No problem," Chris replied, meaning it.

⁓

Dan was happy with the support and reckoned any future coup attempts would fail based on his popularity. He lit another smoke and wandered towards the sound of single rounds being fired from a rifle. He found Steve drilling Leah on their makeshift range, which was framed by high banks on each side and dead ground in front.

Steve had done well, making scarecrow-type targets in-between the trees. As Dan approached, they spotted him and stopped. They seemed to be having an intense conversation, and as he got to them, Steve asked if Leah could demonstrate her current exercise. She beamed at Dan under the weight of her vest, with the G36 hung across her chest.

Dan looked at her for a while before saying, "Continue."

He called Ash to him and walked back a short way.

Steve stood ready with his stopwatch as Leah drove in a lazy circle to come back to the range. As she neared, he yelled "CONTACT" and started the clock. She slammed the brakes on the vehicle and slid from the driver's door to drop to the ground. She appeared under the open door and fired two rounds from the G36 into the closest dummy. One in the chest, one in the head.

She rolled to the side and rose to her knee, where she fired two more into the next dummy. Again, her accuracy was good. She ran forward ten metres and dropped to one knee again. Steve yelled "STOPPAGE" so she dropped the carbine to hang at her chest while she drew the Glock as she simulated a weapon jam. She rose as she fired two more rounds, slower this time but still as lethally accurate, then advanced at a crouch.

"RELOAD. CLEAR PRIMARY WEAPON," Steve shouted.

Leah dropped to her knee again, holstering the pistol.

She dropped the magazine from the carbine and racked the slide three times before seating a fresh magazine and pushing it home. She chambered a round and called out "RELOADED," then stood and stalked to the end of the range using available cover to good effect.

On approaching the final dummy, Steve shouted "AUTOMATIC FIRE," prompting Leah to duck into cover and make herself small. Steve then called "ENEMY RELOADING," and Leah popped out to fire five rounds into the last target.

"STOP, STOP, STOP," Steve called. Leah made her weapons safe and ran back for debriefing. She was barely out of breath.

"Twenty-nine seconds, four enemies down, no injury," Steve declared. Both looked at Dan.

"I am impressed!" Dan said with a genuine smile as he walked towards them. "Why five rounds in the last target?" he asked.

"No clear line of sight for headshot. Four shots to the centre mass until I got line of sight," she barked like a marine corps recruit.

Dan really was impressed; their little girl was becoming quite the capable killer.

"What's your time?" she asked in an innocent voice which oozed with challenge.

He thought about it for a while, then decided to humour her.

"Let's find out," he said, taking the G36 and a spare magazine. He thought through the exercise and decided on a different approach. "I'm not that familiar with this weapon, so that's my excuse if you beat me!" he said jokingly.

He climbed into the Defender, put the seat back about two feet, and drove a loop as Leah had.

Steve called the start of the contact, and Dan accelerated hard to the range. He skidded to a stop and took out the first two dummies with a single headshot as he rounded the Defender's door. He ran forward, and when the weapon jam was called, he fired a double-tap from his Sig into the dummy before taking the position it was in. He cleared and reloaded quickly, then stood and stalked along the left side to the next piece of cover. On being told he was under automatic fire, he took cover and dropped to the floor. The instant the "RE-LOADING" call came, he rose and fired into the head of his last remaining target.

He strolled back to Leah and handed over the weapon. She looked at Steve, hoping.

"Nineteen seconds," Steve said, keeping his face neutral and hiding the smile that threatened to emerge.

Leah looked dismayed. He hadn't done that to humiliate her, she knew that, but she felt like she was being taught a lesson.

"Cheer up, kid. At thirteen, I would've shot my toes off!" Dan said kindly. He bent down to her. "Seriously, Leah, you're good. Really good. Keep it up and you can have my job soon."

She smiled her biggest grin before Steve told her to sprint to the farm and back before cleaning the weapons. She ran away, feigning annoyance but actually very happy.

"There's a big difference when they shoot back, mate," Dan said tiredly to Steve.

"We both know that," Steve said. "I just wish she didn't have to find out one day."

NO ESCAPE

She lay there and coughed all night.

It wasn't a normal cough; it was a deep, chesty cough that racked her whole body into convulsions and went on endlessly, leaving her breathless and weak. Her skin burned and her head pounded.

She cried during the brief respite and tried to breathe in shallow gasps so as not to aggravate the cough again.

Each one was worse than the last, and her heart beat so fast she thought it would burst. She had no idea how long she had been like that; all measure of time was lost in the endless cycle of pain and delirium.

Effectively, that was what happened to her the next day when she was too sick to move anywhere. Others were in the room with her, but they were trapped inside their own failing bodies too.

During a coughing episode, the pressure on her cardiovascular system became so intense that the multiple haemorrhages in her system caused too much clotting for her weakened body to deal with.

She suffered a fatal heart attack and died within forty-eight hours of exposure to the poisoned air.

Two of the group who had been allowed into the bunker – seemingly to rebuild their country and its infrastructure when the infection burned itself out – survived past the forty-eight-hour mark without any symptoms.

The junior medical lab assistant, Emma, sat alone talking to herself. At first glance, you would think that she had seen too much and the trauma had caused her grip on reality to weaken. It hadn't; she sat with her eyes closed and visualised her lab as she spoke her notes out loud into a small digital voice recorder.

"Infection through airborne means is most likely due to the lack of other visible means of transmission. Very fast gestation period, ranging from ten to fourteen hours, death followed within thirty-four hours of visible symptoms to all subjects monitored. Other subjects available for monitoring left the test area during gestation."

She opened her eyes and looked at the array of bodies who had died in front of her as she walked between them, making observations and notes.

"Two subjects out of twenty-nine remain unaffected. Based on the available – and very limited – data, I can extrapolate no common denominator to establish a basis for immunity. Gender, age range, ethnicity, physical size and appearance are effectively opposite in both surviving subjects."

She stopped recording and looked sadly at the other survivor.

The colonel had gone downhill significantly since people started to show signs of infection. He had ranted loudly about being the last high-ranking Army officer left, making him Commander in Chief. He shouted at the bodies, giving his authority to launch tactical missiles at Russian cities immediately before ordering further strikes on China. On seeing the lab assistant watching him, he began to scream that she was a Chinese spy and ordered her to be arrested immediately. She wasn't Chinese – she was part Korean and had never actually been there – but she was sure that it would be a waste of time to explain this. She left him to his solitary war and monitored the others who had not survived.

She took a small rucksack from the possessions of a soldier who would no longer have need of it, collecting similarly useful items from everyone and closing their eyes when required.

She sorted her small pile into order and packed her rucksack, including the blessedly thin and light laptop and its charger, useless without power, knowing that the battery life must be preserved until another source was found. She carefully wrapped it inside a zip-topped plastic bag to protect the contents.

She readied herself to sleep in another room not occupied by dead people. She did not feel brave enough to travel at night, and planned to leave in the morning. She would have to leave the colonel so as not to be shot on sight for the crime of looking a bit Chinese.

THUNDERBIRD TWO

Dan had spent two days scouting and recovering the things he needed. He had found a coach company and managed to start an almost brand-new vehicle which was stored inside a large weather-proof unit.

Ian was recruited to drive it, and it was now parked on the road by the farm.

Steve had found a high-capacity Defender pickup truck, a one-thirty wheelbase with three seats up front. Neil had gone over it mechanically first, then started on the tubular steel work in the back. He had brought Mike in to consult, and a series of flexible rubber mounts were fashioned to stop the machine gun from shaking itself loose.

Dan's additions to Leah's plan involved Steve and Lexi acting as snipers, and for that he needed them accurate over three hundred and fifty metres minimum.

The sights of the newer semiautomatic rifles were swapped out for more powerful optics, and in the absence of heavier weapons, they practised with their new HK416s.

Dan was worried that he would have to rely on Joe to fire the big gun, but Neil was the only person other than himself who had ever even seen one fired before, let alone used one. He told Dan as much, and said he was coming. He would hear no argument against, and

Dan didn't try too hard. He was glad to have Neil with him if this went down.

On their first day of sniper training, Steve declared the 416s to be inadequate. "It's not the accuracy; it's the weight of the round," he explained. "To guarantee a kill at the distance you're looking at, we need bigger guns."

Dan considered the heavier of the hunting rifles, but these only held a few rounds and were bolt action. He thought for a while, then turned to Lexi.

"Clean and stow the HKs and remove the optics. Put the holographic sights back on, please?" he said, then turned to Steve. "Remember that army camp you went to years ago for your E&E training?"

He did.

"Good, we're going in ten minutes."

RETURN TRIP

Dan drove hard as Steve scanned the countryside. Ash nosed his now huge snout through the gap between their seats, and when Steve gave him a sideways look, his tongue slashed out like a viper to drench his face with sticky dog drool.

Steve told Ash exactly how much he enjoyed it and was answered with a short growl. He leaned over closer to his window for the remainder of the journey.

They arrived there by lunchtime, drove straight through the gate and into the camp after a drive-by check.

Dan navigated them between the buildings back to where he found the soldier. He told Steve the story on the way there, explaining that he had wished he could bury the man but had an unshakeable feeling that he was being watched.

He felt much better now he had a well-trained pair of eyes watching his back – not that Ash wasn't good backup, but he had yet to master using a carbine.

"That explains this exotic piece then?" Steve surmised, patting the rare short-barrelled SPAS shotgun resting on the dash where it sat when it wasn't on Dan's back.

They got out of the Discovery quickly as it stopped. Vehicles attracted fire, Dan remembered being told repeatedly when he was younger.

They fanned out each side to find hard cover, scanning all round looking for any sign of danger. There was none, but neither of them fully relaxed.

"People probably know what this place is, and who was based here," Dan said.

"But I doubt they know where they keep the good stuff," Steve finished for him. "There's more guns here than in West Africa."

"I'm happy with these ones," said Dan as he moved carefully forward, Ash stalking by his side, "but more rounds and some heavier toys would be nice."

He followed Steve through buildings, past where the suicidal soldier's boots were still visible, eventually stopping by the unremarkable door of an unremarkable building.

The electronic keypad and swipe card system was long since rendered useless, but brute force was making a comeback. They spent some time using their "master key" to cut a squarish hole in the thick layered metal, planning to use Neil's patented door-opening piece. He hadn't yet named his invention, and Dan thought of dubbing it "the swipe card." He looked at the reinforced door, then at his still attractively unique Discovery. Not wanting to risk damaging it, he suggested that they find a disposable vehicle to use. They took a diesel jerrycan and starter pack on a hunt, both setting eyes on a large Unimog at the same time. Dan smiled; these things would go places which would embarrass their own fleet of Land Rovers.

"Yes please!" Steve said.

He tinkered with it for a while with no joy. They had to drag a generator from the vehicle workshop nearby and attach a long set of jump leads to the battery.

After spraying some flammable engine starter from an aerosol can into the air filter – a trick of Neil's – the huge Mercedes engine barked and struggled into renewed life.

They scanned around for evidence that the noise hadn't alerted anyone, and when they felt comfortable, they turned back to their new addition.

Although technically the short-wheelbase version, this was basically a very capable off-road militarised lorry. They checked it over, and it even had a weapon mount above the three-person cab. The back was like a large high-sided skip, with sides thick enough to be safe from small arms fire. It was filthy, but it was a very good find.

"This is too goddamned cool to leave behind," said Dan.

Steve grinned at him. "Don't you mean too valuable?"

"Yeah. That too," he replied. "Now let's get those tyres pumped up."

They used the generator to power a compressor, having found the tyre pressures indicated on a helpful sticker in the driver's doorframe. There were two spares in the back, luckily. They would never have loaded them without a forklift.

Steve revved the huge engine, making Dan smile again. He slowly eased it towards the armoury door with the creaks and mechanical moans of being unused loud in the air.

It was backed up, and the heavy chain fixed to the towing hitch. On the other end was Neil's swipe card, effectively a folding anchor made of heavy steel.

They posted it through and heard the loud metallic *thud* of it hitting the concrete floor below.

Dan hoped it would hold, as it was designed for slightly less resistance than reinforced steel.

Flashes of his training came back to him: "an expensive door lock is only as strong as the sixteen screws holding the hinges into the wood."

He hoped the chain was strong enough to do the job, as it wasn't wood screws he was trying to break here.

He gave Steve a thumbs up as Steve climbed into the cab of the Unimog, revving the engine and creeping forwards to take up the slack.

Dan ran clear, calling Ash away with him.

The chain clanked and creaked under the growing pressure, each knotted link snapping into place with enough force to sever a carelessly placed finger. Steve gunned the big diesel again and again, until the steel door gave its first sign of weakness. It buckled outwards slightly, at the same time as a large chunk of concrete fell away.

Steve knew what he was doing, and Dan doubted that anyone he knew had the same deft foot control as a helicopter pilot. Steve relaxed the pressure on the clutch slightly, allowing the pressure to ease on the door for a second before he lifted the pedal again, faster this time. More of the door surround fell away with each movement as Steve made each pull faster and harder than the last.

Eventually, with a noise like metallic thunder audible over the huge straining engine, the concrete split and the door fell away with a loud *bang*. The massive vehicle shot forward and bounced on its suspension, then stalled.

Steve tried to fire it up again, but it would only let out a wheezing noise as it refused to turn over.

He got out, full of sadness. Dan felt the same; he would have loved having the truck for a number of justifiable reasons.

Priorities.

They allowed the dust to settle before moving into the armoury. Dan had put Ash in the Discovery with the windows open; he was likely to hurt himself on the rubble but could still sound a warning.

They tentatively entered, searching the dusty air with the bright torches mounted on their weapons.

"Clear," said Steve, who had taken the lead. "Now, nothing silly like a fifty calibre; we need to find a few decent rifles and a boot full of seven six two."

The racks of weaponry in front of him were immense. Row upon row of different weapons, some modified and others stock. Dan took a large armful of Remington pump-action shotguns. Easy to use, reliable, and capable of being used for hunting, blowing door hinges away or cutting bad people in half.

They searched, resisting the urge to take everything. There were so many weapons neither of them recognised, some bearing Cyrillic or oriental markings.

A rack of rifles looked promising, and Steve crowed at their success. He had found three new Mk14s, the American-made enhanced battle rifle with a full-length rail and skeleton stocks. They were part-painted in tan colouring over the black underneath.

These types of rifle had been popular for some time now, designed to bridge the gap between frontline and snipers. A kind of specialist middle-ground killer. They fired a heavy-calibre bullet from a ten- or twenty-round magazine on semiautomatic. Perfect for what they wanted, and lethal up to a kilometre away – if you were skilled enough to put the bullet in the right place. A true sniper took years to perfect the art of long-distance shooting, of studying the physics required to thread the metaphorical needles.

They searched every inch to look for ammunition for them, eventually only finding a few empty spare magazines.

Dan ran his eyes along the racks again, ignoring the weird, wonderful and exotic. He took another few M4s – all that remained in the rack – and put them with his stash of shotguns.

Steve called him through to another room which was decked out like a workshop with bench-mounted tools along one side. There were suppressors and optics lined up, and Steve selected three of the bulbous telescopic sights which amplified light. They also grabbed small bipods, vertical and adjustable foregrips, and shorter-range sights like the holographic red dots on some of their other guns.

Steve grabbed everything he could, excitedly throwing all of it into boxes. Dan carried on until he found the next room stocked with various ammunition types. They filled his Land Rover with crates of heavy ammunition and shotgun cartridges. They filled the remaining space with 5.56; although they had lots of it at home, it would run out eventually.

Steve came back in and saw that they still had a lot more ammunition to take but no space to carry it. He ran back to the Unimog and desperately tried again to start it. He bucked it forwards in gear until it finally caught and started. Dan's joy was short-lived, as it died again instantly and began to steam from under the bonnet.

"It's fucked," said Steve unhappily.

Dan stated that he was well aware of that, then looked at Steve and said, "Trailer!"

They walked back to the vehicle workshop and found a trailer. Its tyres were flat, and they had to drag it closer to pump them up using the generator and compressor. They wheeled it back to the Discovery and loaded all the boxes of ammunition they could find.

On the final sweep, Dan found a box of small suppressors, which he tried to attach to his Sig. They didn't fit, and he looked around the handguns for one that did, throwing everything he could find into boxes. They loaded every crate of ammunition they could find into the trailer until a bark from the Land Rover snapped Dan's attention back to the present.

Dan suddenly felt that familiar sense of dread as he did last time. Unwilling to push their luck any further, he shouted to Steve, "Time to go!"

They drove towards home, eyes constantly scanning for danger.

Their CB was finally in range of the house when they crested high ground about fifteen miles out, getting Leah on the other end.

"You've been ages!" she moaned at them. "People are starting to worry."

"Tell them we're fine, and we will be home soon," he said, driving onwards.

THE HARD SELL

They had brought back so much ammunition that Dan lost most of his room to store it. He thought that maybe it was time he established an armoury in there and move to another bedroom. Maybe there was one near Marie's room.

He forced himself to think productively and not daydream; he had the workings of a plan and the tools to execute it. It needed some rehearsal and fine-tuning, but a lot depended on what the opposition decided to do.

Neil had fitted the big machine gun into the mount and test-fired fifty rounds in short bursts on the range. He showed Dan how he had fitted the metal truck back with rubber loops, allowing him to unclip them silently from inside. He had attached a pole to the front so that when he lifted it, the whole cover flipped over backwards and exposed the machine gun.

Steve and Lexi had stripped and oiled the rifles, and each fired a further fifty rounds to sight their huge optics and practise. They were ready to go at four hundred metres, easily inside the range where the wind or atmosphere would be a serious issue for aiming. At that distance, they would drop a human like they were water. Now came the big problem of convincing the council to endorse his plan, as this was too big an issue to decide by himself.

He called a meeting, having spoken to James and some others in advance for support.

After dinner, all departmental heads gathered at his request, and he laid out the groundwork.

"As you may know, the place where James and Ed were found is under the control of a man who calls himself 'Bronson'. I'm told the name stems from what he does to people who disagree with his methods. I won't bore you with secondhand details of his atrocities, but with your permission, I'd like to bring James in to share some of what he saw." Dan looked around the room, receiving nods all round, and the mood took a darker feel.

He called James loudly by name, and the nervous young man came in.

"Thank you, James," he said. "You know why you're here, so please tell us what living conditions you suffered and what punishments were dished out by this Bronson."

James seemed nervous, but he had been well coached in which bits to highlight. "They kept us in metal shipping containers, in a circle so we couldn't get out unless they lowered the crane to us. That's how they got us out to work and how they put in food and water and the buckets for…" He trailed off.

"What work did they make you do?" asked Dan.

"Fetching food for them, carrying things around; that was the men anyway," he replied.

"What did they make the women do?" Kate asked in a measured voice to control the anger of the obvious answer.

"Cook, clean, and…" James faltered.

"And what, man? Please speak up," said Penny, softening her snap with a reassuring smile.

"Bronson says his boys need entertaining. He uses the girls to entertain them. Some of them bring food and drink back to share with the others afterwards," he finished. Enough said on that point.

"The punishments. Tell us about the punishments," said Dan.

James's face creased slightly. "They'll have punished the others because we ran. I don't know what he would have done, but it won't have been nice. He made us all watch him cut out a man's tongue for shouting at him once. He made another man, a boy really, fight him because he stood up to him to protect a girl. He beat him to death in front of us."

"You say he fed and watered you. Was it enough?" asked Neil, secretly part of the plan to endorse the mission.

"No. Some people fought over it, saying they should have it. A few of those, Bronson lifted out and made them guards. Ed got a few beatings for trying to make sure everyone got a share. When they saw he was big enough to take it, they offered him a job carrying stuff for them. That's how he got me out with him to work where Lexi found us," he said.

"What about your living conditions? How many people are we talking about?" asked Chris, also secretly onside thanks to Neil.

"There were over thirty of us to start with. Three people died in the winter. They got sick and never got better."

"No medical care?" asked Kate angrily.

"No. They thought it might be the bug that killed everyone and didn't let anyone out for a few days," James said sadly. "One girl died of an asthma attack."

Nobody spoke, and Dan asked the council if they had any further questions for him. They didn't.

"Thanks, James. Could you please ask Leah to come in?" he said.

He left, and Leah entered full of confidence carrying a model of the area as described by James.

She laid it on the table and looked at Dan hopefully.

"Thanks, now go enjoy your evening," he said, disappointing her with the dismissal. He didn't want her letting anything slip.

As the door closed, he turned to the assembled heads and asked, "Are there any objections to a rescue mission at this point?" Nobody spoke; he was sure the objections would come thick and fast soon. "This is the area James described," he began. "As you can see, it is heavily fortified, and a stealth approach has been ruled out due to the geography. I propose to visit the camp and speak to the leader. If diplomacy fails – and let's be realistic here, it probably will – a plan to remove the captives by force is available."

He looked at the council and received blank stares from some, nods of encouragement from others.

"This is a big operation and holds equally big risks. I want this to be a vote, but I want everyone to be clear about why I want to do it. Humanity must prevail, and with that we must save people from a system that uses slavery and brutality for the benefit of the few," Dan said, launching into his prepared speech about doing the right thing. "Two of my Rangers will be placed here and here," he said, indicating nearby buildings. "I will approach in a vehicle I have prepared for a confrontation." As agreed, he left out Neil's involvement for now so he didn't seem complicit. Democracy was all well and good, but he liked to hedge his bets. "Should they not release the prisoners, the snipers will deal with the guards on top of the containers. I will have to deal with the remaining hostiles coming from this building here," he said, again pointing to a part of the model.

"How many are we talking about, mate?" asked Chris.

"Up to twenty. I plan to be there at dawn so they will all be inside and probably still drunk," Dan replied with some trepidation.

All part of the plan.

"Can you handle that many?" Neil asked, full of rehearsed concern.

"I'll have to; nobody else can work the machine gun," he said, easing into the sticky part of the plan.

"Snipers? Machine gun?" said Penny. "Is it safe to assume that you plan to kill these guards and Bronson?"

"Yes. I do. It's true that I'm the violent one here, and sadly, that is my skill set. I can't grow things or make things or heal people, but I have used my abilities to keep every single one of you alive. I want to save these people, and I'm asking you all to allow me to take our Rangers and a few others to bring back thirty-plus people who deserve better and to stop a tyrant before he is too powerful to deal with. What if we ignore this now and next year he knocks on our door to take what he wants?"

"It's too dangerous," said Penny. "Your plan is obviously flawed, as you will never have time to use the machine gun if they are watching you."

Neil cleared his throat. "Actually, I'm the only one here to have ever used one. I'll go with you."

"I can't let you do that–" Dan began, but Neil cut him off harshly.

"I was using them when you were still in school, so don't tell me what you can and can't let me do," he said, keeping his face stern and staring Dan into submission.

"In that case, the plan will work much better and faster," Dan said with carefully feigned resignation. He looked to Chris and Kate in turn.

"Yes," said Chris.

"Absolutely," said Kate.

Cara looked apprehensive. "I'm worried people – our people – will get killed," she said nervously.

"I agree," said Andrew with uncharacteristic confidence.

"I don't know. It seems very dangerous to have all the Rangers leave at once," said Jimmy, giving Penny some glimmer of support.

He moved to Penny.

"I'm concerned for the welfare of everyone. It's not just you risking your own life again; if you all go and get yourselves killed, then what about everyone else?" she began. "That said, I could not allow my conscience to rest knowing that we did nothing. You must promise that you will seek a diplomatic solution first, though?"

"Trust me, I will. Are we all agreed then?"

They were.

Dan hid his smile and reminded himself to do some extra washing up for Cara and share a beer with Jimmy for playing their parts. If everyone supported him publicly, then Penny would feel alone enough to argue against the plan in justifiably good conscience.

OPERATION EGGSHELL

"Why is it called that?" Leah interrupted for the third time since he started talking.

"Because we need to tread lightly. Now stop talking over me or I'll tell Ash you're edible," he said, snarling. He loved that sarcastic little girl, but she really knew how to piss him off at times. "Anyway! Thanks to everyone here for volunteering. As you know, nobody will be forced to do this," Dan said as he addressed the assembled team.

Steve, Joe and Lexi at the front. Neil, Ian, James and Ed behind. Leah had nagged to be allowed to go, but Dan had flatly refused. He would be too busy to watch over her, as would the other Rangers. He had to compromise by allowing her to be armed when they went, under Chris's careful eye, as he would be nominally in charge of house protection during the mission.

"You've all heard where we are going and why we are going there, so I won't go over the whys and wherefores again except to say that our purpose is to rescue survivors being kept prisoner. We will be setting off long before dawn tomorrow to be in place by sunrise. Lexi and Steve know their insertion points and will be providing cover throughout. Neil and I will be in the modified Land Rover, stopping short for him to get in the back. Ian will drive the coach with Ed and James to reassure the people we are rescuing, and they will stop a couple of miles short under Joe's protection until called in via CB.

Reminder: there will be NO radio traffic until the threats are dealt with."

He paused to make sure they got the point, repeating the instruction carefully, word for word, out of habit.

"I will drive to the site and talk to them. If it needs to go noisy, I will indicate for the snipers to open fire with a hand signal as agreed. Neil will then unveil the machine gun and I will crawl under the Land Rover screaming and trying not to get shot." His joke got the nervous laugh it deserved. "Snipers will stay in place until extraction, then fall back and regroup at the agreed site before we return home in convoy."

"Just in time for tea and medals," declared Wing Commander Neil.

Penny and the others had not been idle. Bedding and clothing packs had been prepared, and the second-level dormitories were cleared and fresh bedding laid out. Cara had spent the two days since the meeting baking cakes and pastries as Nina maintained the commercial cooking side effectively.

Kate had laid out a triage area and had a set of hospital scrubs ready for each of her team. Marie and Penny were standing by to welcome the new arrivals and organise them with all those not busy on the farms.

"Get some sleep; alarm clocks set for two a.m." He nodded dismissal to the group and turned to see Leah's face set in a stone mask of neutrality, which she had adopted since being told to be quiet.

"What's the matter with you?" he asked.

Leah fixed him with an evilly fake smile, replying in a sweet voice, "Nothing."

Dan didn't sleep, but that was fairly normal for him. Just after midnight, he took Ash outside and then went into Ops and loaded four of the new Remington shotguns which had been stored in his room. Chris would distribute these as he saw fit, and Dan trusted him to make the right choices.

He checked over all the equipment he was taking, but left the personal weapons of the other Rangers, as he wouldn't like someone tampering with his; it messed with a person's chi.

He was restless and ready by one a.m., waiting for the others. They trickled down one by one in silence, but all were early. As they were preparing to go, Leah stumbled in looking sleepy but carrying two flasks of coffee. She must have got up early to boil the water. She gave one to Dan and kept the second for herself, making him wonder when she had started drinking coffee. More bad parenting, he assumed, but wasn't like he had got her an appropriate present for her birthday.

She pulled on her vest and took her Glock and carbine, checking both chambers and making sure they were safe before adding sugar to her drink. That was good: a sleepy teenager demonstrating weapon discipline when half-asleep. He went to go and a grunt from her made him turn back. She walked over and tentatively put her arms around him, unsure of herself. He hugged her back tighter, and she simply said, "See you later", then turned to switch on the CB to monitor their progress.

Dan led the convoy with Neil sitting beside him. He had left Ash behind, not wanting to risk him being hit in the hail of bullets he anticipated or biting a refugee. They didn't speak, save to look behind and say that they still had their convoy.

Lexi and Steve followed, with Ian driving the coach stocked with food and water, and Joe behind. They took the route Lexi had followed, knowing it to be clear, going at a steady speed so Ian could easily keep pace. They went like this for over three hours, until Dan pulled up at the point where Ian's coach and Joe would wait for word that it was safe to move up.

Dan drank a coffee and rehearsed exactly how he wanted it to go, then factored in what could go wrong. Lexi and Steve left after thirty minutes, creeping towards their posts on goggles to save using vehicle lights. He had insisted on radio silence in case the other group had a CB and were monitoring it. Slim chance, but his paranoid way avoided the possibility that they would be the ones ambushed and not the other way around.

Another hour went by and the sun started to creep onto the horizon. His snipers should be in place by now. He felt good to have them there; he trusted them, and both owed their lives to him.

He willed himself to be calm and went over and over the variables. He finally admitted two things to himself: one, he had no intention of allowing this pack of bastards and their psycho leader to live, and two, he realised all the people with him trusted their own lives and that of the prisoners on his ability to wing it.

He looked at Neil, who looked as anxious as he felt inside. "We doing this?" Neil asked.

"Ten minutes," Dan replied, looking at the first rays of sun in the distance.

Ten minutes came and went in silence. Dan started the engine.

Neil quietly recited some part of a speech from *Gladiator* before winking and climbing out. Noises from the back and a gentle double thump on the thin bulkhead between them let Dan know that Neil was ready.

"Show time," Dan said quietly to himself before setting off with his lights on full beam.

MAKE IT RAIN

He arrived at the camp in a few minutes, seeing a dirty multicoloured replica of Leah's white model. He rolled in slowly, saying through the bulkhead to Neil, "Thirty seconds!"

The muffled reply of "Roger" came back with a jaunty roll of the letter *R*.

Dan drove closer just as the sun was up over his left shoulder. He saw a flurry of movement on top of the curious array of shipping containers, then, as the low building to his right came into view, he skewed the nose of the Land Rover to the left to give Neil a better arc of fire.

He got out of the vehicle, wearing clothes that made him not look like himself; he had grey trousers on and a bright-coloured T-shirt scavenged from the camping shop months ago.

He called a "Hello" to the visible guard and received a string of obscene abuse back. He decided to adopt the idiot approach, which annoyed him that people always found believable, and tried again.

Just his luck – Bronson was awake.

Dan was thrown for an instant. He recovered in time to assess the big man walking towards him. He had the inescapable look of an ex-pro heavyweight boxer, and hands big enough to choke the life out of a grown man.

Bronson was intimidating before he saw him, but now Dan was properly scared and considered ordering his troops to open up immediately.

He gathered his nerves and tried to play the idiot for a little while longer.

"Hello there!" he said cheerfully with a faked lisp. "Haven't seen anyone in days now. I'm Eric," he said, offering a hand. He didn't look like an Eric, and Bronson didn't accept the hand.

"What do you want, little man?" Bronson growled. Not many people could say that to him with any degree of accuracy, but Bronson was right. The man was a monster.

Every second Dan waited, the sun climbed higher in the sky, making the targets easier for his team. It also gave time for the other enemies inside to get organised. He decided to speed things along.

"I've heard you have people in there. I'd like to take them off your hands," he said, knowing that without the snipers and Neil, he had just signed his own, and likely very painful, death warrant.

"You want to take them, do you?" Bronson said in a voice dripping with dangerous menace. "Then fucking take them, runt. Right now, or call for the fucking cavalry to come and save your arse, because I will rip you to pieces."

"OK, but I want you to bring your people out to watch me beat you. Fair fight, you and me," Dan replied, feigning a confidence he didn't possess in the slightest.

Bronson smiled at him. "You!" he shouted as he turned and pointed at a half-drunk guard. "Everyone out here, now," he yelled, turning back to Dan with a smile.

Dan began some ludicrous-looking stretches and bounced on the spot like he was preparing for some Victorian bout. He killed maybe half a minute by doing this, hoping to get all the targets out into the killing ground.

As more men began to emerge from the building, Bronson could wait no longer and advanced to get his breakfast.

"I warn you, I'm armed!" Dan said suddenly, showing a demented smile, and then pointed his finger at the beast like he held an imaginary gun.

Bronson stared at his finger for a second, looked at him directly, and roared with laughter.

~

Steve lay prone, the crosshairs of his rifle's sight resting dead-centre on the huge man standing in front of his friend. Dan wasn't a big man, but he certainly wasn't small, and he had a presence which couldn't be ignored. In current company, however, Dan was dwarfed. Steve watched intently, keeping his breathing slow and regulated as the monster suddenly laughed at Dan pointing his imaginary gun.

The corner of Steve's mouth curled slightly in smile before he let out his breath, held it again, and squeezed the trigger with the crosshairs still on Bronson's chest.

The impact rocked him, but miraculously he stayed on his feet. His mouth opened and closed twice, before he slowly turned and fell, exposing the gaping hole in his back.

Bronson was dead; now for the rest of the snake.

Dan dived behind the Defender, going low for the opposite door to retrieve his equipment. Simultaneously, he heard the crack of Steve's first round, followed quickly by the zipping sounds of more bullets homing in on their targets. All he heard was *zip*, *crack*, *zip*, *crack* until a roar of challenge erupted from the back of his vehicle.

Neil heard the exchange. He heard the *zip*, followed by the sickening impact, and then the report of the rifle reached his ears. He unclipped the last rubber straps holding the back down, then heaved the pole up and over to reveal his weapon. He roared as he did so, flung the heavy metal lid away, and racked the long bolt of the gun with his left hand.

"I am the cavalry, bitches!" he yelled, then fired his first burst into three watery-eyed enforcers running from the building.

Dan forced himself to be calm. Methodical. Without his kit, he was a hindrance. He pulled on his vest, tightened it, and then picked up his carbine. His mags were fully loaded, and he had a lucky bullet in the pipe ready.

He flicked the catch to automatic and ran away from the vehicle as he used it for cover. He climbed aboard the large crane sitting a few metres away, then ran up the extended arm to get on top of the containers. He dropped to one knee and fired a series of short bursts at the confused guards who were standing exposed.

One of these was winged, clipped in the upper arm. He spun almost gracefully and fell the fifteen feet into the prison pen where he landed on his back with a *thud*.

Dan fired three more bursts, once seeing his target snatched out of his scope as Lexi's – he assumed hers from the angle of the shot – bullet took the intended victim straight through the lower back and felled him instantly. Dan could hear the steady rhythm of carefully aimed shots coming from the snipers, interspersed with Neil's short bursts so as not to overheat the gun and risk a jam. He swore he could hear laughing from somewhere.

He moved along, taking advantage of the top cover, before the shooting stopped.

Dan had to clear the building fast, before any slackers had the chance to organise themselves. He seated a fresh magazine and racked the gun, then turned the torch on to full, which was blinding in close quarters even in full daylight. He quickly went room to room, finding nothing until he reached the back of the building. He kicked open a door and advanced, seeing a man pull a girl to her feet by her hair. She couldn't have been much older than Leah. The ragged man started to issue a poorly planned threat to make this murderous intruder leave him alone, and died with three bullets in his head and one in his neck.

Dan moved on, slinging the M4 on his back and drawing the stubby shotgun over his right shoulder, as the stairwell was too tight for the carbine. He took the stairs quickly, bizarrely thinking how many times he would have heard "BANG" clearing a house this fast before.

Fuck the lot of them – new manual. Speed was the key here.

The top of the stairs was suddenly filled with a man throwing a bomber jacket on before he froze seeing Dan. The man's blood sprayed on Dan's face as his chest exploded from the heavy shot which sent his body flying backwards to tangle the legs of another running along the corridor. Dan almost fired again, but recognised the body shape of a young woman just in time.

He switched back to the M4 and cleared five other rooms, in the last being faced with what should be a difficult situation of a surrendering man.

One in the chest, one in the head.

He checked each room again and found three women coming out from their hiding places.

He went back to the front door and tied a red strip of cloth from his pocket onto the end of his hot carbine, the agreed signal for *It's me. Please don't shoot me in the bloody head.*

Neil called out to him, saying it was safe. He came out slowly, holding the rag high as he stepped through a pile of broken bodies in front of Neil's smoking barrel.

He turned to where the snipers would be and gave a thumbs up, the agreed signal for *Clear. Stay on post and shoot anything unfriendly.*

He safetied his weapons and went to Neil.

"Twelve!" Neil said, slapping the big gun and instantly regretting it for the mild burn.

"Three up there," Dan replied, pointing to the containers and trying not to think that they were bragging about ending human lives. He considered this for a second and imagined that the girls inside probably weren't there by choice. "Four inside. One point-blank with the shotgun," he finished.

Neil made a pained sucking sound, before delivering an extremely camp "nasty pasty".

Dan climbed into the bullet-holed driver's door and found that of the few shots returned at them, only one had done serious damage. The radio was destroyed.

WHAT WERE YOU EXPECTING... GRATITUDE?

Neil offered to walk back to get the coach, but Dan told him to drive the Land Rover.

"Go steady," Dan warned, knowing that Neil would be full of adrenaline still.

Dan walked amongst the piled bodies, thrown down in grotesque poses by the heavy bullets. Now he had seen for himself what they had been doing, he felt no remorse for attacking them, nor even for ambushing them as they had.

He saw that some carried weapons: bats and knives, a pickaxe handle, even a whip. These were slavers, not survivors. They were dressed and equipped more for taking on a zombie horde than anything else. They weren't survivors; they were tyrants.

He stopped above Bronson's shattered body and marvelled again at the size of the man. Bronson probably would have been capable of ripping him to pieces.

He collected a few shotguns from the scattered bodies and three handguns from Bronson and another now unrecognisable man, thanks to the bullet in his face, checking their pockets for spare ammo. None of the other weapons were much good, and those he had were filthy and pitted through a lack of proper maintenance.

175

Movement in the doorway made him raise the carbine, and he saw two girls in their teens huddled together. They stared at him with red eyes, waiting to see if he were to be their next master. As if to indicate that they would not resist him, one of them slipped the shoulder of her dirty top down to show the skin.

Dan nearly flipped, striding over to them with his weapons out of his hands.

"You don't need to do that. Ever again, not unless you choose to."

The girls looked blankly at him. He gave up.

He stowed the revolvers he had recovered in his pockets and looked at the semiautomatic, as it didn't feel right. He ejected the magazine to find it filled with little yellow plastic balls.

The bastard had been terrorising these people using a BB gun. A child's toy.

A low groan came from a body to his right. Conscious that he was being watched, he put his back to the building and drew his knife without making a show of it. He found the man, a boy really, with two bullet wounds in his abdomen. Neither had hit anything vital, but he was assured of a long death as he bled out in agony. Dan pushed the knife into the side of his neck, twisted it a quarter turn to allow the blood to gush out to the ground, then removed the blade and cleaned it on his clothes.

As subtle as he had been about it, the two girls in the doorway had seen what he did. Neither showed any reaction as they were joined by another woman. Based on her lack of clothing, Dan guessed that she was the one he nearly cut in two at the top of the stairs.

He decided he should address the sounds of excited talking from inside the pen of containers. He climbed the crane again, standing on top of the containers. The sun was higher now, and the murmuring sound swelled as he stood in sight of them. He waited for a question to be asked of him, then remembered that these people had been punished for speaking up before. He would have to say something.

"I come from a group of survivors. We do not keep prisoners. Everyone has a say. Everyone is protected. Everyone is fed properly. We rescued two people and learned of this place, so we came to set you free."

Over sixty eyes were glued to him, but nobody said a word. He could hear engines coming and glanced behind to double-check it was Neil and Ian. He saw the coach first, then the Land Rover in front as they crested the rise to approach him downhill.

He turned back to the dishevelled people in their pen.

"We have medical care waiting at home, and everyone is invited to join us. You would not be a prisoner there; we offer our help."

He was growing concerned that they all just stared at him, and he turned to jump down before a small voice reached him.

"Did you kill them?" a woman asked.

"Yes," Dan said after a brief pause.

The woman's face dropped, and her head and shoulders followed. Others seemed to take this news badly too, but the majority rejoiced.

He dropped down to see Neil coming forward ahead of the coach.

Dan approached him as he stopped.

177

"Think you can work that?" Dan asked, pointing at the crane.

"No, but I can probably drag one of these back instead," Neil answered as he indicated the shipping containers in front of him. He went to find a chain.

Ian pulled up and manoeuvred the coach into position like it was some aid mission to refugees. He supposed it was, in a way. He poked his head into the coach, climbing the first few stairs. Both James and Ed looked sick, whether that was from the bodies they stared at or being back in this place, he couldn't say. They hadn't wasted their time; each seat of the coach had a blanket, bottle of water, an energy bar, and other snacks.

Neil was rigging the chain he found at the crane to the towing hitch of his vehicle, having secured it to the corner of a container. He planned to drag it back at an angle which would put it flush against the one next to it and leave a gap where they could file out towards the coach.

Dan gave him the nod and the tyres bit into the rough concrete, hunkering the truck down on its springs. The container inched along, making a painful noise as it ground backwards, leaving deep scores.

The gap opened enough for a person to get out, but nobody came. Wider still, enough for two, and still nobody ran from their prison. Dan waved Neil to stop, and then walked into the circular compound. Everywhere people hid, as others stood still in the open. He realised these people were more damaged than he expected.

"It's not a trick," he yelled at them. "You are free and we are offering you shelter, food, medicine and protection."

A few nervous people shuffled on their feet, before James and Ed came into view. People recognised them and another ripple of low talk went round.

James ran in, heading straight for a container and shouting a girl's name as he went. He came back out into the growing light, leading a young woman. The migration started slowly as people followed those led by James and Ed. Then people jostled for position at the gap. He saw three people run as soon as they were out in the open.

He knew they didn't trust him, so he did not try to stop them. *Good luck to them*, he thought. He watched the girl James was leading as she stood over the broken body of Bronson, pure hatred in her eyes. She spat in his lifeless face.

People brought what meagre possessions they had and filed onto the coach one by one. Some talked, but most were silent. Dan walked around their prison, seeing the way they had been forced to live. He eventually set his eyes on the guard he had wounded and knocked into the pen. His head had been bashed in and was almost completely flat. What was most worrying though was the empty holster at his waist.

HUMANITARIAN AID

Dan told the others about the missing gun. It concerned him deeply. He remembered training for hostage scenarios, where the hostage takers would hide themselves as victims. He had a terrible feeling that there was a wasp amongst the flies.

He walked along the coach, wanting to draw the Sig and search each person. They tore hungrily into the water and snacks, barely giving him a glance. Those who did look at him had eyes full of suspicion.

He didn't have time for this; their one-sided gun battle would have been audible for miles around.

"We've got to get moving," he said as he strode to the front.

He had to trust that everyone knew what to do and led the coach back up the road past where they had waited. Joe had set up at the rendezvous point already. He watched the road ahead as Neil got back on the big gun, watching behind.

Dan walked along the aisle of the coach again, looking for any subtle hint that any of the passengers were hiding something…like a gun.

It was useless; they all looked edgy and all but a few gave him looks that made him feel sick. They were waiting to see what tortures lay in wait from their new captors.

One man had the courage to speak up. "Where are you taking us?" he asked.

Dan spoke loudly for the benefit of the others. "We're taking you to our home. You can have a hot shower, clean clothes and a warm bed. You'll have medical care and a proper meal."

Some regarded this news as too good to be true, and the mistrust was plain on their faces.

"What do we have to do?" asked a woman.

"Nothing," said Dan. "I hope you will want to stay and be a part of the group, but I promise you that you will not be captives. If you want to stay, you can find work to do, but you should all gather your strength and get better first."

He hoped that they would trust him; any show of strength on his part would put him in the category of those who had imprisoned them.

Lexi arrived next, holding up four fingers to Neil in answer to a question Dan hadn't heard but easily guessed what they were talking about. That made twenty-three.

Steve drove up a short time after, and Dan saw his lips mouth *five* as he pulled up by Neil.

Twenty-seven, and only twenty-five bodies. Dan told himself the miscount was due to multiple people aiming at different targets. He was sure none survived, but without Ash or a team of forensic experts, he would never know.

They formed up again, and this time Dan took Lexi's Land Rover and went up front with Steve. The coach rode in the middle, then Joe and finally Lexi driving with Neil still manning the big gun.

Twice the rearguard stopped and planned an ambush as the coach and lead vehicles went ahead slowly.

Dan tried the CB in Lexi's Defender as they neared their home turf, finally getting through nearly twenty miles out.

They made it home in three hours, where the welcoming committee was ready.

DAN'S HIGH COMMISSION FOR REFUGEES

The coach pulled up and the doors opened. Nobody came out.

Dan jogged to the front door of the house as people were coming out and he stopped in front of them. "They aren't the trusting type," he said, "and I think one of them may have taken a gun from a guard. Everyone be careful and send for me if there is any trouble."

Kate went into the coach, wearing her old paramedic uniform for added reassurance. "My name is Kate, and I am in charge of medical services. My team will see everyone to take care of you. There will be hot showers, clean clothes and food. Please follow me," she said and then turned away.

Slowly, people started to emerge cautiously after James led the girl and encouraged the others to follow them.

One by one, the scared, ragged survivors filed towards the house. A conveyor belt system had been organised, where survivors gave their name to Karen, who was established on a desk in the reception area. Others were standing by to issue clean underwear, trousers and tops, as well as a plastic bag containing basic toiletries and a towel.

James led the girl to Karen, still holding her hand. She was thin, dirty, and had dark rings around her sunken eyes.

"What's your name, sweet?" asked Karen kindly.

"Pip," she said in a small voice, wild eyes scanning desperately.

She gave her age and her former occupation, then shook her head when asked if she had any other skills. Kate led her straight into medical as soon as she was given some clean clothing.

As the pattern was established, so too the pace picked up. Their suspicions were slowly being eroded as the promises were made good.

Dan left Penny and the others hard at work sorting the new people into small groups where they were led to the bathrooms.

"Please keep the showers short for now. We don't want to run out of hot water," Carl said as he took a group of three men upstairs.

Dan saw his Rangers loitering around their gunship with Neil.

He walked to them, as he didn't want a string of heavily armed troops walking past the traumatised intake.

He had let Ash out, keeping him very close despite his interest in all the new people who may feed him. He recognised Neil and bounded over, receiving some treats hidden in his leg pocket.

Dan lit a smoke and offered one to Lexi. He inhaled deeply, eyes closed and head upturned before letting it out slowly and blowing a plume of smoke over their heads.

"Fucking nice work, people," he said at last. He looked at Steve and asked him how his perspective went.

"Took some trouble getting in place to start with, and had to move to a closer building and climb the stairs to the roof," he said. "Perfect line of sight, and I had that big bastard in my scope with you ready for the signal. When it went loud, I dropped three on the containers where they sat, then covered the windows as you went inside, taking a runner from the building after you went in."

Dan nodded approval, worrying that he had missed one when he went inside. Five for five, 100 per cent.

He turned to Lexi.

"I got on target easy enough, but the height advantage wasn't enough to get an angle on you and Neil. I took four out as they came into view on the containers. One miss," she said.

Dan guessed that she had been the one to snatch his target from his scope but figured this wasn't the time to argue over the hunting etiquette of whose bird it should've been.

Neil chimed in after. "I heard dozy bollocks here challenging the Sasquatch to a boxing match and unclipped the back as quietly as I could. I saw the guy go down through a slot in the side, then jumped out of the cake like a stripper."

He feigned taking offence at the intentionally invited giggles.

"There were half a dozen standing around the big guy, waiting to see him kill someone. It was sick, like a playground bully with no teachers to run to." Neil got serious then. "They went down before they had a chance to figure out what was happening. I took seven down in the first two bursts, then another five as they ran out. I didn't hear it, but one bastard emptied a revolver at me. I saw him aiming as I was taking down a runner and saw the muzzle flashes. Look!" he said theatrically, and held his shirt out to the side.

"What?" said Dan, looking for the point of his show.

Neil poked a finger through a small hole running through his top twice. "It's a good job I'm thin," he said, joking.

With anyone else, Dan would worry that he was in shock and that the panic of nearly catching a bullet in the stomach would affect him. Not Neil: he genuinely found it funny.

"Good news is," Neil went on "Thunderbird Two here worked perfectly. Mike's rubber mounts were the key, I reckon."

Dan agreed. Without the big machine gun, there would undoubtedly have been losses, probably himself. "Good job, you lot," he said.

Before he could continue, Steve asked, "What about you?"

He paused, then said, "You saw it. I pulled up and that Bronson was the one to greet me. I played dumb and offered to fight him for the survivors. I knew he wouldn't be able to resist the chance to show off, and he sent someone to fetch his audience. Then Steve ended his reign and I grabbed my kit, taking three on top of the containers."

"What about inside?" Steve enquired gently.

"Four more. Stairs were very tight, so I had to use the shotgun. One came at me on the top of the stairs and I hit him in the chest at close range. Damn near cut him in half."

The gruesomeness of this revelation hung heavy for a few seconds before Dan snapped himself out of it. "Quiet as you can, guns into Ops and clean them. Neil, just stow the belts for the GPMG for now. And everyone, keep sidearms on you until we're sure we haven't brought back anyone dangerous. I want to be sure no foxes ran home with the hounds, if you get my meaning."

They took their leave, and Dan brought his own guns to his room, where he cleaned them and locked them away, keeping the Sig. He left Ash in his room, now more of an ammo store than his quarters, and went to see how the high commission for refugees was faring.

He opened his door to the sight of Leah holding a cup of coffee to him, smiling. He accepted it, thanked her, and said she could put her guns away now. She seemed a little put out, so Dan explained that these people had been kept prisoner by armed guards and he didn't want to look like that was the case here. She understood.

He took his coffee to the dining hall, flanked by his eager apprentice, and saw lines of freshly washed people wearing a collection of new clothes, mostly prison tracksuits. In hindsight, maybe not the best things to put them in, but it would have to do for tonight.

Cara was greeting the new arrivals, explaining which way the impressive buffet went and inviting them to get a plate and join the queue which led to Nina dishing up large helpings of pasta bake.

Cara and her team had outdone themselves with the spread, which included a long table full of pastries and cakes. Andrew was probably having kittens somewhere over the amount of extra supplies they had used.

There were cans and bottles of sweet drinks, even cartons of cigarettes and lighters left out.

The people seemed more relaxed and had even started to talk amongst themselves quietly. He felt a few cold looks from some, but he joined the line for lunch. Three times he had to refuse being offered to jump ahead of those who clearly needed it more than him.

He sat with Leah aside from the others. None of them joined him until a freshly showered Pip sat down a few seats away. She hesitated before summoning up the courage to turn to Dan and offer their thanks. She seemed like she wanted to say more, but didn't.

"You're welcome, Pip. It's good to have you here safely," he said quite loudly, eager to show the others that he wasn't guarding them.

He could guess from her interaction with the former Bronson how she had earned her food previously.

That was what offended him the most about the way life had become after it happened, like the Mad Max twins and the country boys. Some people were just waiting for the bigger players to leave before they threw their weight around and took advantage of others. Sure, they were surviving in their own way, but what good was the human race without humanity?

REVERSING THE PAVLOVIAN EFFECT

It took days for most of the thirty-one survivors to adapt to freedom. Some of them had been captives for months, others only a week or two. The brutality they had lived under was terrible, and Dan could only guess at the damage done.

The downside of this was that they had effectively taken in thirty-one mouths to feed who were all weak, malnourished, injured and scared.

He knew he wouldn't be lucky enough to have found a couple of special forces reconnaissance soldiers, and the thought lingered on how many of those they had killed would have been offered positions as Rangers if they had been found here instead.

That led to the thought of how many of his own would have become enforcers if the scenario were different. He pushed that thought from his head. The answer was simple: none. None of his would act like that, not even to save their own. It wasn't right, and using violence was not the same as what had been done to these people. At least, that was the theory he swore by.

Slowly, they began to integrate. After a week, Maggie took ten of the new arrivals and taught them the basics of the gardening side. Another five accepted work on the farm for Chris. One group of eight kept very much to themselves, almost a split faction. Dan kept a close eye on those.

Pip insisted she earn her keep but was outright refused by Kate, as she found her in very poor health. She told them that she had been pregnant when it happened and gave birth to a stillborn baby in their makeshift prison.

James hung around her like a moth, but Dan saw he was annoying her and sent him back to work with Pete. He slipped the old gamekeeper a half bottle of Johnny Walker red label and asked him to keep the man very busy and tired. Pete gave a conspiratorial wink, and true to his word had James out until very late netting rabbits, then up before dawn to deal with them. He kept him out hunting overnight at least once a week.

The ringleader of the separatist front approached Dan one day as he smoked. Ash didn't like the look of him and made that clear with a low growl. Dan told him to stay, and he lay on the ground, never taking his eyes off his master as he walked away with the stranger.

His name was Martin. He was a thin, pinched-looking man with a permanent scowl. He started with some insincere thanks for the hospitality, but he struck Dan as a man who hadn't unpacked his suitcase. Dan listened in silence; his dad had always said to let the other person fill the silence and only speak when you had something important to say.

Dan stopped and turned to him. "I'm not a man to piss about, as you have probably guessed. Make your point, please."

Martin straightened himself and asked permission for him and the other seven to leave.

"You don't need my permission, but you will need my help," Dan said. "Where do you plan to go?" he asked.

Martin was clearly annoyed that he was being asked to tell this man his secrets and said nothing.

"Let me guess," Dan said, "you're either planning to hit the coast and take a boat, probably south for the continent, or you know of a place where you can set up by yourselves."

Martin looked uncomfortable and a little embarrassed. "South of France," he said finally.

Dan took his time finishing his cigarette, then looked at him directly. "I told you all that we were getting you out of there. We fed you, we fixed you, we clothed you," he explained. "At no point did I say that any of you had to repay that, even though we risked the lives of everyone here to do so. I'm not rubbing it in. I'm stating facts," he finished.

Martin said nothing.

"Speak to your friends tonight, then find me after breakfast tomorrow. We'll help you plan your routes, your equipment, teach you some things you may not have learned, and find you a vehicle." He turned away, leaving a shocked Martin nervously clutching the stolen gun in his coat pocket.

Martin let it go and wiped his sweaty palm on his leg, worried that it was too easy.

The following morning, Dan emerged to take Ash outside. He hadn't even had a coffee before he went back inside to find Martin waiting for him. Dan held up a hand and asked for five minutes, visiting the toilets and the kitchen for a pot of coffee before he returned. He poured a cup for Martin, not bothering to ask if he took milk or sugar. All of his team drank black coffee, probably because he did, although he was sure Leah probably had a stash of sugar somewhere.

Martin was invited to explain their plan. They wanted to head for the southwest coast, where one of his group had a sailing boat. They planned to get there, stock up, and sail for France, where another of them had a gîte near the coast.

Dan asked what supplies he needed.

"A few days' food and water, nothing else," Martin replied.

"Maps?" Dan enquired.

"A road map would be helpful," Martin answered.

Dan stood and took a gulp of coffee before selecting an unused A3-sized road atlas book of the United Kingdom. He dropped it on the table in front of Martin and offered rucksacks and sleeping bags as well as some other basic equipment to see them to the coast. They should do that in three days easily, even given the degraded state of the roads and the risk of banditry.

Martin still looked at him suspiciously before blurting out, "What's the catch?"

"No catch. None at all. If you want to go, then good luck. I'll find a minibus or a pair of vehicles for you today to leave in the morning," Dan said.

"Honestly?" Martin said, his face pleading.

"Yes. While we're on the subject of honesty," Dan said, backing a hunch, "don't you think you'll need something better than the little handgun you've got?"

Martin's face told him he was right.

"Show it to me," Dan instructed him.

Martin reached into a pocket and carefully produced an ancient small-calibre revolver. The thing would most likely fire, but you'd have to be holding it to someone's head to kill them. He checked the cylinder – four rounds, practically useless.

Dan made a judgment call. "We have a rule here: nobody carries a gun unless trained and authorised. By me." He spun the gun gently around on the table. "You'll get this back in the morning, along with a good pump-action shotgun and spare ammunition. It's easy to use and maintain. You'll have a vehicle by then, you have my word."

Martin had been played into a corner, and he had little choice but to trust the man.

Leah wandered in shortly after to find Dan sat at the table with a pathetically small gun. She gave him a puzzled look and a greeting.

"Morning, kid. Kit up, we're going to buy a car."

193

YOU BREAK IT, YOU BUY IT

Dan took his Discovery, the now familiar three heads riding along looking out at the world.

They took spare fuel and a starter pack as they headed to the coach company where they found the rescue vehicle. Inside, they practised the building clearance in a real situation. Dan was very happy with Leah's technique but unsure if she had the maturity to make a challenge and maybe shoot someone if she had to.

They selected a sixteen-seat minibus and set about getting it started and fuelled. They used a cigarette-lighter pump to inflate the tyres and left it running to settle the disused engine.

Dan asked Leah if she had a D1 category on her licence. She was confused and unhelpfully pointed out that she didn't have a driving licence.

"Well, you're going to have to drive mine then," he nonchalantly declared. Her face slowly broke into her characteristic grin where she tried to hide how excited she was.

"You're OK with the automatic gearbox now?"

She was. She had been watching his movements as he drove for months. "Yeah," she tried, as coolly as possible.

"You sure? Because the last time you tried, you crashed into a forty-grand convertible, if you remember," he said, enjoying goading her.

She smiled sweetly. "True. But now I know how to strip that weapon you're holding in the dark. People change."

Once again, he couldn't argue with her logic.

He held the keys out to her but held tight to them as she tried to pull them away. "Don't. Crash. It," he said firmly.

"If I do, I'll get you a new one for your birthday. When is it, by the way?" she asked innocently.

"Bugger off."

They set off back home, Dan driving the minibus up front with Ash riding in the passenger seat.

He looked in his rearview mirror. There was a thirteen-year-old driving a nearly sixty-thousand-pound, three-litre diesel, off-road car. If that wasn't bizarre enough, she was driving it well and carried two guns which she knew how to use.

The following morning came and went. The council had wholly agreed to allow the group to leave; the unanimous decision was that to prevent them would be to imprison them. They supported the minibus idea and they were given extra clothing as well as basic camping supplies. Dan had kept his word and returned the tiny revolver to Martin. He had also included a stock Remington with no attachments and showed the group the basics of operating and cleaning it. He added a box of ammo – hunting cartridges, but still quite a heavy load.

They left and life moved on easily enough.

DEAD WEIGHT

Penny called a council meeting that evening. She had been a rare sight amongst the occupants of the house in the last few days. For that matter, she had spent a lot of time in bed recently. She passed it off as just being a little under the weather but refused all offers of help from Kate.

She saw her personal matters as exactly that: personal.

She was in a bad enough mood as it was, and the pains in her belly were crippling some days. She knew it was something serious, something that needed doctors and hospitals and expensive machinery to take scans that consultants would meet and discuss. She walked into the meeting with her own dark cloud hanging over her, and her feelings made themselves known a little too strongly.

"We have eight people here who are not contributing," she started, holding up a hand to stop the few protests she saw forming. "I know one of them is unwell after being pregnant, which is a passable excuse for part-time employment, but that still leaves seven who are a drain." She went to continue but was hit with a wave of pain from her stomach.

Kate took the opportunity to jump in before the rant started again.

"I'll stop you right there, Penny," she said acidly. "The girl is malnourished and has been badly mistreated. It's a miracle she didn't die in labour, and that's taken a toll on her body. She stays close to me and my team at all times, not negotiable, and as for the others, they are also physically very weak. I've got two in medical right now if you cared to check."

Penny winced, fought back a cry of pain, and sat down.

Kate stood and continued. "That leaves five frightened, damaged and abused people who aren't ready to work a chain gang for you, so you can–"

"Kate! Enough," snapped Dan, not because he disagreed but because he saw the pain hidden in Penny's eyes.

"What? You're on her side?" Kate asked angrily.

"No. Look at her!" he said as Penny stood with some difficulty and turned to leave the room.

Dan stood too and only just made it in time to stop her from cracking her skull on the steps to the door.

Kate barged him aside to check her. Typical paramedic: she did everything she could to save a life regardless of what she thought of the person.

Kate called Penny's name and was rewarded with a faint squeak through shallow breathing. Penny's eyes screwed shut and her body went into spasm as the pain overtook her again.

Kate looked at Dan with wide eyes, and said "Trolley". He ran to medical, ignoring the worried looks from those he thundered past, returning with the ambulance stretcher and raising the panic levels further.

Penny was wheeled through, and the shouted names from Kate ended the free time of her team. Dan followed and had the door shut in his face. He turned to the assembled crowd and tried to act blithe.

"It's OK, everyone. Just let them do their jobs," he said with a smile he was sure was as fake as a gold Rolex from a market stall.

He maintained the TV-presenter face as he strode into the dining room to find the council still seated, bar two members.

"Meeting adjourned, I think. Unless anyone has anything else?" he said.

If they did, they had probably forgotten it now.

FIELD PROMOTION

She guessed she was now the senior lab assistant, as there were no other candidates. She theorised with herself as she walked, reckoning that a cure was a little pointless now, but finding out the cause could be useful.

She spoke into her digital recorder again. "Theory: what if the virus mutates? Could natural immunity be beaten in this way? Are there any other effects of exposure to those immune to the lethality?"

She stopped recording, running the numbers through her head.

"Assuming a ninety to ninety-nine per cent non-immunity, based on available data, further mutation could be assumed to result in similar lethality, with an eventual population effect of point one per cent."

She paused, unsure if she should theorise further without a more senior scientist to check her work. She told herself she was the senior scientist, probably in the whole country. So she recorded what she believed.

"A viral mutation would effectively eradicate the population of the country without a rapid reaction to bring all surviving humans into a controlled breeding programme. This would almost certainly require outside organisation. If the virus has spread worldwide, which must be assumed based on the transmission being believed airborne, then planetary population by humans is unlikely within a generation."

Serious shit.

She walked on, looking for alternative transport to walking even though she had prepared herself by running on the treadmills every day.

"You're like a hamster on a wheel," the Chief Researcher used to say to her. "Maybe we should use you as a test subject." He laughed, thinking it was funny. He was a sexist, racist pervert. If things were normal she would have written a formal complaint to the university that employed him. As it wasn't, she had to tolerate his endless sick joke of waving a five-pound note at her and asking for a happy ending.

Still, he was dead now, and she didn't mind one bit.

She walked on, planning to find a vehicle and enough supplies to get her on the way to the other site in Scotland. Their virology data would advance her theories one way or another.

Travel light and keep moving, she told herself. *Avoid contact with others in case of viral mutation.*

THE FRAGILITY OF LIFE

Penny was weak. The pain racked her in waves, taking her breath away. She wanted to tell someone. People said that sharing problems halved them.

Did that mean they believed that if she told someone then her cancer would shrink by half? Stupid thoughts by stupid people.

In the end, she had to tell Kate. The paramedic had seen the scars. Being a paramedic, she had learned to guess the surgery from the location and size of the operation scars.

"Penny," Kate said softly, "when did you have the colonoscopy?"

Penny cried gently as she told the story of how the pains started and how the consultant had wanted to operate quickly. She had tried to refuse, saying that she was too busy at school to take months off to recover. The consultant had told her straight: no operation meant no chance of survival. She had the operation, leaving her deputy head in charge for nine weeks before she dragged herself back to work. She had put off the follow-up appointments, then it happened and there were no longer any doctors left to prescribe her course of chemotherapy. She was dying, and she knew it. She wept into Kate's arms until she fell asleep.

Miles away, Kyle also wept pitifully. He did so in silence so they didn't beat him again for being soft. They brought him out every so often, making him crawl like a dog with a lead around his neck. Soon, they said, soon he would lead them to his old home where they would take over what the others had built. Then they would give him a new kennel, they laughed. Kyle wished he were dead, but he lacked the courage to invite it from them or do it himself.

STEPPING DOWN

Penny asked to speak to Marie. She came straight away, thinking it was an emergency of conscience. Penny explained what she wanted of her, and extracted her promise to keep her word.

Penny called again for a council meeting that evening, a week after she had collapsed. She was helped into the room by Kate.

She thanked them for coming at short notice and promised to keep the matter brief. "I had bowel cancer last year. It was removed by operation, but I believe it has returned and will soon be the end of me." She looked at the assembled faces, registering shock and fear. Kate had clearly been good for her word on confidentiality. "I fear I am of little use to everyone as I am, and it will only worsen for a short time until," she paused, swallowing, "until I'm no longer with you."

Tears began to show on her cheeks, mirroring the silent crying from others around the table.

"It is my wish that my seat on the council be passed on to a worthy candidate, effective immediately. To that end, I propose that Marie be considered for Head of House. If any of you have an alternative suggestion, please make it now."

She tried to veil the tiredness she felt, but wanted nothing more than to lie down.

Nobody suggested another name as she looked at each face in turn.

"Very well. All those in favour?" she said, forcing a smile.

All the assembled raised a hand.

"My other wish is for people to start having babies," she said, throwing out a shocking revelation. "Thank you for indulging me," she said with a smile. "Now if you'll excuse me, my doctor insists I rest."

Kate helped her from her chair as the council watched her walk slowly from the room.

One by one, they rose and left without a word, deep in their own thoughts.

UNBURDENED

Dan went to Penny the next day at her request. He thought he should have brought a gift or something, seeing as she was in hospital and terminally ill. He said as much to her and she dismissed his frivolity. She asked Kate to give them some privacy, which Kate did without a word.

"I wanted to speak to you, for my own peace of mind," she said weakly. She was propped up in bed and looked drawn. Pale.

"What do you want to know?" Dan asked, guessing what it was.

"Tell me about yourself. Who you were before, I mean," she asked.

"I think you know some of it," Dan said, stalling.

"I believe you were a military man. Maybe a policeman after that," she said with a smile.

Dan smiled back. "Right on both counts. I was a Royal Military Policeman, then I joined the regular police after I got out."

"Why did you leave?" she asked.

"Boredom," said Dan honestly. "I wanted a family and I didn't want my kids born and raised on some drab camp in Germany. I was sick of fighting with pissed-up squaddies, so I left."

"And what then?" Penny urged, her smile wavering with a sudden pain.

"I started again from the bottom, which wasn't fun, but I got married and had two kids. Emily would be seven now, and Michael would be four." A single tear dropped suddenly from his cheek, soundlessly hitting the sheets of the bed and soaking away to nothing. Penny gripped his hand reassuringly. "They weren't with me when it happened; they were with their mother. None of them made it. I was too upset to bury them." Dan's head dropped and the tears flowed freely as he let go of the stress.

"You were separated?" Penny asked gently.

"Divorced. Long story," Dan said with a mirthless laugh, cuffing the tears away from his face.

"Will you make me a promise?" she urged him.

"What's that?" he replied.

"Speak to Marie," she said with a tremor of passion. "She can help you."

Dan nodded, not entirely certain he would keep that promise.

"You had nobody else?" she asked.

"Parents. Didn't speak to them much because of the divorce and the stuff before. I think they blamed me. I had a girlfriend; we hadn't been together too long, but she died too."

"What happened before?" she wanted to know.

"Oh, that is a long story," Dan answered.

"Tell me," she asked with a squeeze of his hand.

Dan told her. Told her everything. He told her of the guilt, the fear and pain of what he went through which led to the divorce and all the hurtful revelations that came with it.

When he looked up, he saw that Penny had drifted off to sleep with the pain medication and the exhaustion of her illness. Part of him hoped she hadn't heard him, that she wasn't burdened by his secrets and his pain. He hadn't spoken about it for almost a year, but he did feel better to have shared it.

Dan stood, wiped his eyes, and put back on the mask he hid behind every day and left quietly.

NORMAL SERVICE RESUMED

Penny died in her sleep ten days later, kept comfortable in medical with liberal pain medication. Dan suspected that Kate had helped speed things along with the morphine. He never mentioned it but liked to think that she had and was grateful for it.

She was buried during a small ceremony, in a patch of woodland overlooking the lake where bluebells grew. Everyone sat through a sombre evening meal before Dan broke out a few bottles and poured lots of glasses.

He stood on a low table in front of the television and raised his glass. "To Penny," he said, holding his glass up as tears rolled down his cheeks. The assembled survivors, a true cooperative society as envisaged by the few he first brought together, echoed his words.

The following morning saw the mood no higher, and routine tasks were given out. Dan sent Lexi and Joe out together to gather all the how-to books they could find in a library not far away. Neil made a fuel run with Steve running protection, and a logistics team went with them to clear any more supplies still in date.

Mike had continued with the solar power project, having requested the rest of the warehouse contents be brought back. Two scaffolding towers sat proudly in the space that now saw sunlight, as Jay had cleared almost a dozen trees with the help of some of the newest recruits. Dan had never learned their names, other than Pip, who grew healthier by the day. Pip had loved to read before, she said, and set herself up in the library where she read and sorted the books into order.

Mike and Carl were busy providing electricity to the farm, with further plans to do the same for the gardens. That included the cottage on the edge of the now blooming walled utopia.

Maggie and Cedric spent a lot of time there, having cleared it out piecemeal. Dan was invited to look at it when he stopped to see their progress one day. It was a lovely place with a large garden and three bedrooms. They had hot water there, courtesy of the solid fuel burner. With electricity, they would have power to the large shower in the wet room.

Their formal request to live there permanently came in spring and was agreed to by the council. Before Dan could raise objections from a safety perspective, Marie asked if they were not overly exposed and without protection. Their firework alarm system was extended and a CB radio was to be installed in the house as well as the gardens themselves. Dan also insisted that Cedric keep possession of a Remington shotgun and ammunition. These caveats satisfied, they moved in as soon as their solar panels and additional hot water tank were fitted.

They were probably the happiest people there. Even happier than Leah, who had become bored with endless training and no live deployments. Even after he had explained that no matter how good she was, she wasn't going out alone until she was older, Dan's thoughts of getting her a short-wheelbase Defender were shelved for now, despite him having recovered the right vehicle. He didn't want to risk a teenage strop where instead of going to her room and slamming the door to play loud music, she took a vehicle and automatic weapons.

In truth, her accuracy and range drills were second only to a few. She could spar well; removing knives from would-be attackers was easy for her. She was fit and strong, but still he couldn't allow himself to send a child out to fight on his orders. He loved her like she was his own child, which in a way she was, and his feelings of responsibility made him hold her back.

The farms and gardens were producing fresh meat, eggs and vegetables. Soon there would even be salad. In fact, the only department to be under strength was Ops. One of the refugees saved was very ill when he came to them, but when he healed, he formally requested an interview with the "OC Operations". Dan showed the written application to Steve, who also recognised the military jargon for Officer Commanding.

The man was sent for immediately, and Leah found him helping in the stores.

He knocked before entering, despite the door being open, and Dan stood with Steve as he said, "Come in."

Dan extended his hand to the man, who was standing rigidly to attention.

"At ease, man!" said Steve, playing the second in charge perfectly.

The man relaxed a fraction, allowing his shoulders to drop an inch. He was tall but very spare, like he had been starved. Dan put him at about thirty, but the worry lines in his face could be betraying a younger man.

He hesitated, then went to shake Dan's hand, displaying his own, which was missing the two smallest fingers and part of the hand. Thick burn scars were visible on his right arm and at his neck.

Dan sat, inviting the man to do the same. Three cups of coffee were poured by Leah before she returned to her desk and tapped away at her laptop, pretending not to listen.

"What's your story, soldier?" Dan said as he blew in his drink.

The man looked at him, realising he had completely given himself away.

"No, sir," he said, offended. "I was a Royal Marine. Corporal."

"In that case," said Dan, "accept my apologies, and call me Dan. At the most formal, I accept 'boss' from my lot."

"OK, Dan, I'm Richard. Rich if you like."

The marine saw Steve looking at his hand. "Helmand. Pyrotechnic IED. Got me sent home with two boxes that used to be my mates. Last man only survived because us three took the brunt of it."

Dan nodded, lost for empty words often used to pacify someone's sacrifice for a now utterly pointless loss. He had met a few people injured by improvised explosive devices, and knew that the scars ran so much deeper than the visible layer.

"After that?" Steve asked.

Rich sagged a little. "Medical discharge. Six weeks' counselling on the NHS for the PTSD. Then the booze. Wife left and took the money. Ended up homeless for a time."

"And then you were captured?" Steve asked.

"Yes. Captured and beaten. I hurt one of them badly when they took me. They woke me," he said simply. Waking a soldier by surprise was one thing, but startling a Royal Marine with PTSD was another entirely.

"Tell me about your time there," said Dan in an interested tone.

"I was sick a lot of the time. No booze. Made me bad for weeks," he offered. "I let myself down. In my day, I could've taken that Bronson character."

Dan doubted him slightly on that. "So," Dan said, "how can I help?"

The Marine Corporal straightened in his seat, becoming more formal. "Sir. I'd like to offer my service to you," he said.

"It's Dan," he said patiently, "and I've got some concerns."

"I'm off the drink; that's the only good thing to come from that," he said forcefully. "I let myself down, and I need to make up for it."

There was fire left in the man. Dan saw that and he wanted it, but not at the risk of others.

"Maybe so, but there are other issues you will need to address. Namely the PTSD; what if I gave you a gun and the first time you heard a bang it set you off?" Dan asked rhetorically before continuing. "We have a counsellor, and you will see her twice a week until she gives me the clearance to give you active duty."

Rich nodded.

"You will also undergo physical training until you are fit, and I warn you, she," he said, pointing at Leah, "will outrun and outgun you now. She's thirteen." Leah smiled as her pretence of being busy cracked. "Her mile and a half is down to nine minutes and her range scores are almost as high as mine. After that," Dan said, "you can work from here manning the CB and cleaning weapons. You'll be our quartermaster until we are both independently satisfied of your return to active-duty status. So, tell me, Marine, are you still interested?"

Without hesitation, Rich replied, "Yes, sir."

"It's Dan. 'Boss' to my lot at best," he repeated patiently.

"I'm in, boss," Rich said, looking him directly in the eyes.

Dan offered his hand again with an accompanying smile. "I'll let you know where to be then, Rich."

ANY EXCUSE

Like an excited boy, Dan went to find Marie. He felt a bit pathetic and exposed when he spoke to her, but this was a perfect excuse for some alone time.

He found her room door ajar, and knocked.

"Hello?" came the voice from inside.

"It's Dan. Are you busy?" he said, trying to sound casual.

"No, come in."

He walked in to find her sitting on her bed reading a book. She pulled her glasses down her nose and regarded him warmly. They had seen more of each other since she joined the council, and he liked that.

"How can I help?" she asked. "You haven't shot someone again, have you?"

"Funny," he said. "No. I've just had a rather damaged Royal Marine ask to join, and I need your help."

Marie put down her book and patted the bed next to him. He hesitated and she said, "Do I smell?"

Dan blushed and mumbled that she didn't.

"Have you brought your wolf?" she asked mockingly. Ash seemed to betray him utterly with her and played the puppy when she called him.

"No. Just me," he said quietly.

"Well, come in then."

He sat with her and explained the meeting he had just had with Rich. He realised halfway through that she must know some of this already, and in better detail, but he carried on with his story to cover the fact that he was sitting in bed with a woman he found irresistible but aloof.

"So, can you work with him twice a week for the PTSD and the alcohol issues?" he asked.

"Yes, but I want you to promise he won't have a gun until I say he's not likely to kill himself with it," she said.

"Agreed," replied Dan.

"Good. Now, where were you based?" she questioned him lightly, surprising him with a subject change.

He rose from the bed, concerned that he was being analysed. "Thanks for your help. I'll send Rich to you soon," he said from the doorway as he turned to escape.

"Hey!" she snapped lightheartedly. "Come here and sit down."

With no idea why, he did as he was told.

"Now. I know you were in the job, so tell me the rest," she said as she closed her book and took off her glasses.

He told her some and she extracted the rest expertly. He didn't tell her everything, though – he wasn't ready for *that*.

WHAT NEXT?

A few weeks later, Dan and Marie took a walk around the grounds of the house.

"It's not so much the PTSD," Marie explained. "It's more survivor's guilt but hugely intensified."

"We've all got some of both, to a degree," he reasoned.

"True, but what most of us don't have is massive underlying trauma like Rich does. Think about it: he's maimed, he sees two friends die in front of him, his career is over. All of this after years of active service. That's just the beginning; he then goes into self-destruct and spirals into a completely different person."

"Hence the wife jumping ship, as they do," Dan interjected bitterly.

Marie raised an eyebrow but let it slide – for now. "Yes. He's alone, and the only thing he has to do is replay the bad things over and over. I'm amazed he's still alive," she finished.

"So the question remains: will he get better?" Dan asked.

She thought for a few seconds, not about the answer but about the explanation. "Yes. In actual fact, our situation may bring about an almost complete absence of symptoms given the right stimulus," she said.

Rich was a unique story to start with, even before it happened. She firmly believed that he was a natural survivor; he'd been shot at, blown up, burned, crippled, abandoned, abused and beaten. Still he refused to give in and die.

She explained all this to him and suggested that a gradual increase in responsibility for him alongside careful progress of talking therapy would give him a purpose. "With duties, responsibilities and a reason to get up in the morning and be useful, he will get better quickly. As to the long-term effectiveness of him as a soldier, I simply can't say yet."

Dan thought on what she had said. "So you agree that he should follow a daily routine of physical training and rehabilitation, then be given more responsibility in Ops without being armed and sent out?"

"Exactly," she said. "I'd like to see him every other day. If all else fails, then repeating 'it's not your fault' at him will at least do some good."

"OK then," said Dan, and he walked along in silence next to her. He liked spending time near her, and selfishly used official reasons to capitalise on it.

Ash loped from the trees to his left, effortlessly sliding towards them. He nuzzled his huge head into Marie's crotch, making her squeal and tell him off for being a dirty bastard.

Dan smiled, keeping his thoughts private.

"So where do we go from here?" she asked wistfully, stopping to light another cigarette.

He did the same. "We let Chris and the others do what they do; within a couple of years, we should be almost self-sufficient. Andrew is happy enough with the stores, without the unexpected arrival of another twenty-three people to feed, that is. All in all, we're doing OK, but we still need to stockpile as much as we can to survive half a

217

dozen winters. I know it seems a bit childish, but I want to stockpile more weapons too; bullets won't last forever, so we either learn to make them – which is dangerous and difficult – or we have alternatives for the future." He finished his small speech and stood there in silence.

"That's cute," she said, "but I meant us as in you and me, not us as in the whole group."

Heart thumping and colour rising in his cheeks, he didn't know what to say. She filled the silence for him by kissing him lightly on the lips.

"One condition," she said seriously, drawing away, "that beard's got to go!"

MAIN SEASON

Spring was in full flow, and the farms and gardens were full of activity from breakfast until evening.

Lambs were born, which meant that Chris and Ana lived in a caravan they had towed up to the farm so that they were on hand to help the ewes give birth.

The garden team under Cedric and Maggie had adopted a routine of planting new crops weekly to try and ensure a steady supply of fresh food without wastage.

Scouting missions went out, with Dan and Steve taking Leah on a few to keep her boredom levels down. There was very little training left for her to do, and Steve suggested testing her E&E skills soon by seeing if she could make it home while they hunted her. Dan thought that was a good idea, but it needed fine-tuning, as he didn't really want her to kill him by accident.

The pigs raised a difficult question, and Kerry's biology and genetics knowledge paid off. They marked their herd according to the family tree she had created. To ensure they didn't have inbred livestock, the piglets from last year were separated to keep a couple of boars ready for the breeding programme, mixing the different breeds of pigs to create their own hybrid. Three generations were deemed enough to prevent any unwanted side effects, and the plan was checked over twice; they had enough variety to breed and sustain a herd for the future.

Luckily the bull was young and had plenty of years left in him. The future of the cows was dependent on finding another one at some point. Some joked that he had the best job of everyone there.

The egg collections had been stopped, and the chickens had become broody. Soon a multitude of fuzzy yellow chicks were running around making peeping noises. Ewan had reinforced the fences with extra layers of tight mesh and then requested the help of the Rangers. Dan and Steve spent the night awake on the farm using their suppressed carbines with ambient light optics.

The following morning, they proudly displayed the ranks of six dead foxes for the Welshman.

Ewan was happy, and the carcasses were swiftly skinned and fed to the pigs before anyone more squeamish saw them.

Dan's freshly shaved face was noticed, but not commented on. He realised how lazy he had become, having spent months just using a set of clippers to trim his whole head every few weeks.

He finally moved his room upstairs, after stubbing his toe for the last time on the boxes of ammunition stored in his draughty quarters. He gave up and moved into what was the Governor's office. The big desk was moved to a corner and the filing cabinets went into medical; there were still plenty of spare rooms, as the offices had been cleared out. He moved his double bed in, and soon found that someone else was adding some more feminine touches occasionally.

He had given up his old room to be a proper armoury, using the cupboard in Ops as the store for the farming and hunting weapons.

Rich had got himself into a routine, going for a run before breakfast. He had asked for a wetsuit and was taken on a scavenging run. He added a swim of the lake to his fitness regime, which others had taken to copying. Within a few weeks, he seemed much better, both physically and mentally. Dan decided to officially declare him recruited on a restricted basis. He spent his days sorting the armoury out, as there were still bags of weaponry taken from various places that had not been sorted. Leah took him to their clothing stores and pointed him towards the black section.

Dan had asked him to show Leah all the weaponry and check her skills at cleaning and maintaining them. This served not only to keep her busy with a new skill, but on Dan's request, Rich spoke freely when he could of the horrors he had seen during his service. He still wouldn't talk of the incident that took two people he knew like brothers and left him crippled, but his descriptions of dead Taliban were detailed enough to remove the romantic thoughts in her head about what she was training to be.

He watched them from the doorway one morning, sitting at a bench with a rack of guns in front of them.

Rich pointed at one, and Leah recited the statistics.

"Heckler and Koch 416 carbine, police model which isn't fully automatic. Fires NATO five-five-six from a thirty-round mag."

Rich moved on to other weapons, receiving similar reports. When she hefted the full-length Remington shotgun with a pistol grip, she looked ridiculous. Rich heard Dan's small laugh and perked up.

"Boss. Didn't see you there," he said.

"I was just looking at Nikita here carrying an artillery piece," Dan replied, smiling at the girl.

She had been given the book, but he doubted she had read it yet. In reply, she stuck her tongue out at him.

Rich stood, bringing a new weapon from a shelf across the room. "I thought you might be interested in this," he said, handing it to Leah and nodding at her.

"Walther P99. Nine-mil parabellum, semiauto, fourteen-round mag," she parroted.

"In itself, nothing that special," said Rich with an echo of the professional soldier he once was, "but it's the only weapon which fits these," he finished, twisting a short suppressor onto the end of the gun. He showed Dan an empty chamber to prove that the weapon was safe, and handed it over.

It felt a little top-heavy, as he was used to the weight of the short Sig, but the suppressor was a very useful addition.

He turned it around, weighed it in his hands and checked the action. The gun felt good in his hands. Solid and chunky. "Any spare mags?" he asked.

"Thought you might like it," Rich said, smiling, and he produced two spares.

Dan loaded the weapon, keeping it pointed at the floor. It felt good. He put his Sig on the table and tried the Walther in the holster. It was a universal one and needed a slight adjustment, but the nearly silent weapon fit OK.

"Nice," he said, "I'll take it!"

"You might want to take a look at these too, then," said Rich as he gently tipped out a box of attachments and sorted through them before he found the stubby torch attachment to fit the gun. He offered Dan an extended magazine, but with the suppressor on the end and the mag sticking out the bottom, he may as well be carrying the shotgun. Dan also took a holster designed to slip inside a belt which was custom-made to fit the weapon.

Something casual for the weekends.

Dan left his Sig for cleaning and stowing, and took the new toy with him. "Keep up the good work," he said as he left them, "and grab Neil when you see him to ask about reinforcing these windows now I'm not sleeping down here."

From outside the doorway, he said, "Oh, and Leah?"

"Yeah," she answered slowly, fearing that he was setting her up for a joke at her expense.

"Driving assessment tomorrow," he said before walking off to find Lou and trade for more needlework. She tweaked the holster perfectly to draw more from under his left arm than across his chest. He preferred that, and it left extra room for two more pouches: one to take a small notebook and pencil and the other the perfect size for a box of twenty and a lighter.

The world turned, the sun rose and fell, and progress was made.

BURN THE L-PLATES

A driving lesson from Dan was not a relaxing experience. He rattled on and on about gear changes and how to assess a bend and what to look out for and what certain things meant. He seemed to forget himself sometimes and told stories of car chases and spectacular crashes, but when she asked him more, he clammed up. She guessed he used to have an exciting job before it happened, but he wouldn't tell her any more about it.

He made her talk him through checking the vehicle over first, explaining everything she should look for and the reasons why. Dan always drummed into her that she shouldn't just be able to perform a skill – she should understand why she was doing it.

"If you only know one way to do something, then you're already out of options," she mimicked back to him during the time he had spent training her.

She gave a good rundown of the vehicle: a Defender 90, in a deep metallic red colour with chunky tyres and a big bull bar on the front. It wasn't modified like some of the others, but she had heavy tow ropes looped on both bumpers. She didn't know it was hers, and Steve had thought he was funny by sticking learner plates in the rear window.

She got in and depressed the clutch before starting the engine, going through all the checks she was taught. The first part of her assessment was done on the roads around the house and farm before she drove to the gardens. Dan made her drive into the narrow sections between the greenhouses and polytunnels to practise her manoeuvring in cramped areas, and she performed well.

He took her out onto faster roads and made her push the speed up. Her reactions and observations were good, but Dan still offered pointers for improvement. He forced himself to be quiet and objective. She saw obstructions and assessed them well, especially when Dan made her drag a car out of the way as though it was blocking the road. She connected the tow rope securely and reversed her Land Rover away under control.

He took her over rough terrain and watched her technique critically. He couldn't really fault her, but then she was just replicating what he had shown her.

She drove him back to the house after over an hour and Dan gave her the final test.

"OK. Imagine you've got a flat tyre. Change the wheel," he said, pointing at the passenger side at the front.

Leah hesitated. She got the tyre wrench from inside the back door and tried to loosen the nuts on the spare wheel mounted high on the back door.

She struggled, eventually removing them, but she couldn't lift the wheel down without risking damage to the wheel or herself.

It finally dawned on her that she wasn't physically capable of doing it, and she sagged with the failure.

Dan rested a hand on her shoulder kindly. "Don't worry about it for now. We'll have to figure something out," he said.

Leah wiped a tear away from her cheek and nodded. She went inside and Dan put the spare wheel back on, feeling bad for disappointing her. If she couldn't do the most basic repair, then it wasn't safe for her to go out alone yet.

THE LEAH SHOW

Dan felt bad for her. She had learned so much and trained so hard only to be denied her independence because she was too small to change a wheel.

He couldn't, in good conscience, let her go out alone. What he could do was take her on a run and be her backup.

A food run was planned. They had to go much further afield now, as they'd picked clean the supermarkets within a short radius of home. With the distance being longer, the danger increased. Other than that, it would be business as usual: two scavenging trucks and a Ranger escort.

Their target was on the outskirts of the city to their north, about as close to the fetid population centre as he dared go.

Jimmy and Mark were in one lorry, with Laura and one of the Bronson survivors in another. Dan's feelings of shallowness returned briefly as he again realised he didn't know half of the people who relied on him and his team for protection.

He told Leah that she was on the protection team for the operation, making her day but trying to sound casual about it so as not to be seen to be throwing her a sympathy party. He justified the additional firepower by making a point about the proximity to the city.

She loaded up her G36 and took three spare magazines. She tried to be casual about it too, hiding her excitement at a live deployment well. Right up until Dan threw her the keys to his Discovery.

She drove well, leading the convoy north with the huge head of a slobbering dog over her left shoulder. Dan had to tell her to keep her speed down to take the pressure off the following heavy trucks. It took them almost an hour to reach the target, and on instruction, she drove slowly into the car park. No recent signs of activity were evident, so Dan called in the others to wait as they cleared the shop.

They forced open the sliding doors and stalked in, crouching low. Even Ash mimicked the search pose, dropping his body weight like a panther as he sniffed the ground. He was restless. He didn't like something he smelled. His low growl was interspersed with a throaty whine which Dan hadn't heard before.

"What's the matter with you?" he asked the uneasy dog as they checked each aisle and found the shop devoid of life.

Ash continued to whine and even let out an uncharacteristic bark. Dan wasn't impressed, as he'd worked for hours on keeping Ash silent when on the job. His instincts were to trust the animal, but his eyes told him there was nothing there. Literally, no sign of human life at all.

He ignored both the dog's and his own instincts and put Ash back in the Discovery after they had cleared the shop floor. They returned to do another sweep and found a fire exit wide open after they passed through the plastic curtains leading to the stock room.

Dan and Leah came back outside and called the others in to clear what was left. Only about a quarter of the contents were of use anymore, the rest having spoiled way beyond salvage.

The four scavengers moved fast. Most bizarrely, Jimmy used a handful of pound coins to release trolleys for them to use. Why he didn't just cut them away with bolt croppers amused Dan greatly. Jimmy liked those small intricacies of life.

Ash barked again from the inside of the 4x4 and the muted sound made Dan turn.

"What's wrong with that bloody dog today?" he asked Leah.

She shrugged and turned back to the shop.

Ash whined and scratched at the windows, unseen by the absent Dan. Movement in the car park made Dan turn and watch in sudden alert silence before his frantic barking started again. Dan came back out into the car park, striding angrily towards the car and the ill-behaved animal.

A scream rang out from inside the shop. A scream of pain and fear, somehow guttural and primeval. Ignoring his ballistic companion, Dan turned on his heel and sprinted for the entrance.

GONE TO THE DOGS

Leah was unsettled by Ash's behaviour. She had never seen him act like that, but Dan had locked him away, so obviously it wasn't an issue. She trusted Dan's instincts.

He should have trusted them too.

She walked along the aisles, looking for anything of interest as the others worked hard stacking tin cans into the bags for life in the trolleys. She reached the section where the bakery had been, expecting to find the bread and cakes rotted away as in the other shops she had seen.

Only they weren't. They weren't there at all. The packaging had all been ripped open, leaving a mess of torn wrappers on the floor. She froze, trying to figure out what she was seeing. She couldn't make sense of it: why would people have ripped it all up like that when they could've just opened it?

The scream cut through her pondering. It cut through the very air like a serrated blade.

She hoisted her weapon and sprinted the three aisles to where the noise had come from. She was met with three of the team all looking terrified.

Jimmy was the only one to be switched on.

"Mark!" he said aloud, counting the only one of them not there. He automatically discounted it being Dan, unless he was the one to have elicited the scream from someone else.

Another scream, slightly further away, and this time it continued in panic and pain.

Leah ran towards the sound. She later realised that, deep down, she was that kind of person. People always said, "Oh, if that happens I'd do this…" They reeled off their actions to any given scenario, not realising that they would probably do the complete opposite. Very few people had the natural instinct to run towards danger when every fibre of your body wanted you to flee and protect yourself.

She reached the end of the aisle and turned. What she saw would stay with her forever.

Mark was bleeding heavily and jerking like a float on a fishing line. The jerking and the bleeding were caused by the four or five – she couldn't be sure because they moved too much – dogs that were ripping him apart.

They were ten metres away, and as she let out an involuntary cry of shock, two of them looked up at her. They were filthy, mangy, cruel-looking creatures. The one nearest her was a thin Staffordshire bull terrier, and it still wore a ragged collar once put around its neck by a loving owner.

The yellow eyes fixed on her as it let out a savage snarl. Along with another rangy-looking mongrel, it launched itself at her, feet scrabbling desperately for purchase on the shiny floor.

Leah reacted. Most people would freeze or scream in terror. Most people would get killed by the pack of wild dogs. Most people weren't carrying weapons, however.

She dropped to put her right knee on the floor as she raised the weapon and flicked off the safety all in one fluid movement.

BANG. BANG.

BANG. BANG.

The force of the launch had given the squat terrier a terrible momentum, which served no purpose other than to propel its dead body across the ground, where it slid to a bloody stop against her left boot. The mongrel had been stopped in its tracks metres away by her second double-tap, but the other three paused in their attack of the now silent Mark and stared at her.

Dogs weren't supposed to do that, she thought, losing valuable seconds of reaction time. They were supposed to be scared of loud noises.

These dogs weren't.

They had banded together, more natural a reaction than the cohesion of their own group of survivors. The reason this area was devoid of signs of looting was because of this vicious pack of killers. They tolerated no intrusion into their territory, and they also wasted no meat.

The two dead dogs represented a significant change in opposition number to Leah, she reasoned, as she lined up to kill the other three.

What she didn't know was that the five she saw were only the advance party.

She heard growling and the noise of claws on the floor, making a swarm of clacking noises as more of the pack attacked from behind her.

She flew to her feet.

"Climb!" she screamed at the three dumbstruck scavengers. They scrambled up onto the shelves, her last trailing limb only just getting out of reach of the snapping jaws. "Dan! Dan!" Leah bawled, not out of panic but to warm him to get off the ground.

They were trapped on wobbling shelves, a horde of ferocious teeth hungrily flowing below them and making attempts to jump to reach the intruders.

Leah tried to turn and kneel up, but the shelf wobbled too much. Afraid of falling into the mass of murderous teeth below, she carefully shifted her weight in an attempt to bring the weapon to bear on the wild animals, all the while bawling Dan's name.

CRY HAVOC

Dan ran in, hearing the two controlled double reports from Leah's gun.

How could I have missed something, he thought angrily to himself, cursing his mistakes for putting the others in danger.

He heard strange noises as he ran through the shop. The snarling, snapping and barking from a multitude of canine mouths was unmistakable.

Leah's voice calling his name cut over the cacophony.

"I'm here!" he yelled back.

"Climb!" she screamed. "Get off the fucking ground!"

Bizarrely, he wanted to admonish her for the language. That such a thought could force its way to the front of his mind was ludicrous given the situation. He leapt onto a low chiller unit and used his hands to pull himself to the top where he could stand.

The scene below him was hideous. He guessed about thirty dogs swarmed en masse around the next aisles, desperate to reach their quarry. He could see Leah wobbling on top of a stack of tins, pushing them to the floor in an effort to stand up without falling. The others were similarly perched in a precarious way, trying to stay flat and not fall to a terrible death.

He flicked the safety catch to automatic and stitched the mass of dogs with four long bursts, killing maybe ten and emptying the magazine. He reloaded and looked for more targets but was blocked by the shelves between him and his friends. He moved to the end of the refrigerator he was on, twice slipping in the dust and grime out of sight from ground level. As he reached the end, he saw Mark – not that he could tell it was him from the blood – crawling away with difficulty.

Three dogs peeled away from the pack and made their way towards the prone Mark, excited by the movement. Dan fired into them, not wasting time by picking individual targets but just firing until they stopped. He was trapped; he couldn't reach the others without getting down, but to do so would invite more targets than he could fell.

Desperately, he looked over to see Leah finally gaining purchase and pushing up onto her knees.

Leah's heart was pounding her blood around her body with more force than she had ever known. Her hands shook from the adrenaline, making her movements ungainly and clumsy as she manipulated her weapon to bring it to bear on the besieging pack.

She fired bullet after bullet into the pack just as Dan had, without picking targets. She fired the remainder of the magazine and almost fell as she twisted to free a replacement from her vest.

She righted herself, breathing as steadily as she could before resuming her methodical execution of the animals. She fired, aimed at another dog, fired again and switched her aim to see a dog flinch and snarl in pain as it was struck by a tin can. She flicked her gaze sideways, following the reverse trajectory of the missile to see Jimmy hurling cans at the monstrous dogs before resuming her executions.

After she had killed almost half of them, a single loud bark sounded. As one, the pack turned and fled through the plastic curtains and out of sight.

Dan had emptied his magazine on full auto into the fleeing dogs, taking down another eight or ten as they ran.

"Are you OK?" he shouted blindly to her in desperation.

She looked at the other three with her, two still frozen in fear on top of the shelving. "Fine here," she shouted back, her voice cracked with terror. "Mark's down," she said.

"He's alive," Dan yelled back, unsure how long his condition would remain that way.

A few stragglers still roamed the shop, growling as they paced angrily, having been denied their kills. Before the thought could make its way to Dan's mouth, Leah shouted to him, "We need to move before they come back."

He couldn't agree more. "On me!" he yelled as he jumped down and dropped to his knee to cover the door where the pack had gone.

Tins cascaded to the floor as Leah marshalled the others down. Jimmy came first, now holding Leah's sidearm and scanning with wild eyes. Leah held the rear, scanning for the marauding animals and walking backwards in a semi-crouch as they approached the bleeding mess of their friend.

"Get him up. Move!" Dan said, the panic making his tone more threatening than he intended. They dragged Mark to his feet. He groaned in pain but didn't seem to be bleeding out; it was pure luck that they hadn't ripped open an artery.

They moved towards the entrance in a bubble, Leah looking forwards and Dan looking back towards the stock room.

Movement flashed all around them as the wild dogs slipped between the aisles to stalk their progress. The dogs had lost most of their pack and were wary.

Wary but hungry.

"Hold!" said Leah as they reached the threshold to the outside world. She took careful aim and fired a series of calculated shots at the few animals who had made it out the back to cut off their retreat.

More movement showed at the rear of the shop as the dogs poured back into the aisles.

"We need to move!" Dan called to her without taking his eyes off the targets. He was forced to aim along the barrel, as the distance was too short to use the optic. He fired at shapes, only hitting one as they stalled in the entrance.

"As one, keep together," Leah answered as they crept painfully slowly towards the safety of their vehicles. To break formation and run would be to invite the animals who hunted them to attack again. Sticking together was the safest way to move, but it was also the most frightening.

They reached the rear of the first truck, and Jimmy hoisted the roller door for the other two to load the bloodied Mark inside. They climbed through the window into the cab and were told to start the engine and wait.

The remaining three made their crablike way to the other lorry where Jimmy climbed in first.

Dan and Leah followed, giving instructions to drive them close to the Discovery to save a panicked dash across the tarmac.

Ash was beside himself with impotent fury. His spittle had soaked the inside of the window and steamed up the van as he had barked with intensity watching the scene unfold. Dan couldn't risk him getting out; as good as Ash was, even the remaining dogs of this pack would tear him apart.

Dan forced his way in, keeping a tight hold on his livid dog. Leah climbed behind the wheel and took off at speed, the two lorries following suit. The pack chased them for a few hundred metres until outpaced by the machines.

After a mile of Leah setting a fast pace and checking the mirrors, she stopped abruptly. She grabbed her bag and piled out, telling Dan to drive. She climbed into the back of the first truck and pulled down the shutter as the convoy got underway again.

It took three quarters of an hour to get back, during which Leah worked on cleaning and dressing Mark's wounds in an attempt to stop the bleeding. Not a single limb had been left without deep puncture wounds, the worst being on his hands and his upper left arm. She staunched the flow of blood as best as she could, talking to him the whole time to try and keep him conscious. She held his legs high in spite of being constantly buffeted by the moving van.

By the time they got back, he had faded. The grey pallor and clammy feel of his skin denoted his descent into shock.

Unbeknown to her, Dan had the sense to put the medical team on alert via radio.

His message of a dog attack didn't even begin to convey the severity of the near miss they had just experienced.

Laura drove straight to the entrance and stopped hard, sliding both Leah and Mark along the bed of the lorry. The shutter burst open to reveal Kate with a stretcher. Hands grabbed at Mark and pulled him out where he was wheeled away for treatment.

Leah sat back on her feet and stayed kneeling for a minute as she caught her breath. Blood-soaked dressings littered the truck, and as she followed the blood trail in reverse from the door, she saw her hands and arms were red with sticky blood as it congealed on her skin.

Disgusted, she got to her feet and felt the pins and needles tingle her legs in pain. She jumped down, almost losing her footing as she landed and fell into Dan. She was exhausted from the adrenaline, as well as from the stress and the physical effort.

Not in the mood for talking, she pushed him away without making eye contact. "Next time, listen to Ash," she said as she walked towards the house, rubbing away her tears of anger.

IT'S ALWAYS WHEN THE DOG DIES

Mark survived. He was in medical for a fortnight and needed fluids and a significant donation of blood. The injuries weren't too severe on the whole, but the infections rampaged through his body, leaving him skeletal and weak. His eyes were sunken and his skin took on an unhealthy tinge, but he lived, albeit horribly scarred.

Sera's knowledge was as important as Kate's when it came to his treatment. Knowledge of the diseases that feral dogs could carry probably saved his life as she suggested the best ways to counteract the illnesses he suffered.

He didn't blame anyone, despite Dan blaming himself, as was his manner. Mark never even knew the dogs were there until he was pulled to the ground. Most of what followed seemed like a bad dream to him now.

Leah's mood evaporated quickly. The first thing she did was to go straight in the shower as she stood, washing the blood from her clothes and equipment as well as scrubbing it from her skin. She dressed in clean clothes and sorted her gear out before finding Marie and crying her heart out.

People were fine. People were the enemy – bad people, anyway. She wasn't at all prepared for the primeval fear of being hunted for food, and that had scared her badly.

What had upset her more was that she had killed so many dogs.

"They were pets, or at least they used to be," she had said after the tears had stopped. She joked that Dan had said in films that the bit that always made people cry was when the dog died. Not the people – that was part of life.

She reasoned that it could've been much worse, reeling through a long list of what ifs before she stopped.

"It happened, though," she said as much to herself as to Marie. "We could have all died, Ash too, but we didn't, and it was down to me."

She hugged Marie and left to find caffeine. Marie sat in silence; the girl had been there for almost an hour and had done all of the talking. She had come in tears but left as strong as ever. Probably more so. Marie was amazed at how quickly the girl could sort and compartmentalise events. She was strong.

Leah walked into Ops wearing clean combats and a black T-shirt with a gun at her side. Dan was sitting at the table looking over a map with Jack as she entered, her emotional outburst seemingly forgotten.

Dan nodded to Jack, who subtly took his leave.

"You OK, kid?" Dan asked the girl as she poured herself a coffee.

"Fine now," she said, a little embarrassed about earlier.

She sat down opposite him, waiting to be told she couldn't go out again. Quite why she was expecting it, she didn't know, but in truth, she wouldn't feel fear like that again if she were forced to stay put.

"We'd have come off a lot worse without you today," he said, surprising her with praise instead of grounding her. "Mark would likely have died, and I doubt we would've got out without being attacked again if you weren't there. You did well, thank you."

She put her drink down and regarded him for a few seconds. She was happy with his praise and had already dealt with the incident in her own mind – that she would have nightmares about dogs was as yet unknown to her – but to hear Dan saying that she had saved his life in a roundabout way was pleasing.

She shot him a crooked smile.

"Like I said," she told him, "next time, if the dog sounds off, we walk away."

"Agreed," said Dan, meaning it.

LIFE IN BLOOM

It wasn't long before Ana announced that she was pregnant. The news caused excitement amongst the group, and when the subject was raised in the council meeting, Cara gave her own admission with a red face.

Both Chris and Matty were to be proud fathers.

Kate gave a groan at finding her team responsible for midwifery, although she had been expecting it at some point. "Has anyone delivered a baby before?" she asked.

"Loads," said Chris. "More than I can count," he admitted, prompting silence from the gathered heads of department who could not believe he had kept such skills from their knowledge. "I never said they were *human* babies…" He trailed off lamely, receiving jeering comments at his poor humour.

EPILOGUE

Kyle was dragged out of his kennel and walked into the building where they beat him, initially for information then afterwards for entertainment.

The leader told him to sit and stay.

"Good dog. Do you know what we're doing tomorrow?" he asked in a voice oozing with threat.

Kyle shook his head, looking at the floor.

"Tomorrow, we're going to go and meet your old friends."

Kyle tried not to cry. If he cried, they would hit him again. He thought of the others there: Lexi, Penny, the kids. He tried not to think about what they would do to them.

He cried in silence, despite his fears.

The story continues in AFTER IT HAPPENED BOOK 3:
SOCIETY

A message from the author

Thanks for reading. Please leave a review on Amazon if you enjoyed it!

You can find me on:

Twitter: @DevonFordAuthor

Facebook: Devon C Ford Author

Subscribe to my email list and read my blog:

www.devonfordauthor.uk